The Fringe Candidate

The Amberica Series, Volume 1

Brad Swift

Published by Porpoise Publishing, 2019.

The Fringe Candidate
The Amberica Series Book One
by
Brad Swift

———————

A RACE AGAINST EVIL . . . and time

— Delivering a simple truth can be the most courageous act —

— Exposing evil rulers is a game of life or death —

Led to the brink of destruction by its corrupt POTUS, Amberica is bleaker than ever. Who could hope to unseat Oscar Wellian, a fascist who wields the full force of martial law? Plenty are willing to try, but only one entrant has what it takes to give Oscar a run for his ill-gotten gains. Enter Angeline Tarkington . . . the people's final hope.

Despite her heart of gold and concrete ideals, it won't be easy. Is Tarkington's integrity enough to combat systemic corruption and heal a hemorrhaging nation? An amalgam of corporate interests known as 'The Triumvirate' will stop at nothing to silence her, and Tarkington can't expect victory without sacrifice.

Tarkington's ability to transform those around her will be put to the ultimate test, as new allies may mean the difference between victory and defeat, but who will join her? In any case, she'll need to tread very carefully. Unmasking a monster will be an invitation to an all-out duel, with the nation as the prize.

With *The Fringe Candidate*, Brad Swift offers readers a picture of untold possibility. The Amberica Series is visionary fiction from a dreamer's apex—dark and doubly daring for its optimistic soul.

Acknowledgments

I WANT TO START BY acknowledging the two women who were my inspiration for writing The Fringe Candidate, my wife, Ann, who has been my staunch supporter in all my crazy endeavors and especially on this one. I also want to thank Marianne Williamson for stepping up against all the odds to run for President of the United States. It was her courage and her message that led me to create the imaginary world of Amberica, where the transformation of politics isn't only a possibility but actually happens. I encourage all readers of this book who are not aware of her efforts to bring love, kindness, and compassion to politics to check out her website at www.Marianne2020.com[1].

I also want to thank Sharon Ford and the incredible people of the Landmark Living Powerfully seminar in Greensboro, NC. Your continual stand for what's possible made this book possible. Thanks also go to my Beta Reading Team and my Amberica Series Launch Team for giving me valuable feedback on the book and helping to spread the word about it. And thanks to Scott Searle, my editor, and BetiBup, my book cover designer.

---

1. http://www.marianne2020.com/

Part One - The Gathering Storm

Prologue

WHO SAYS GOD DOESN'T have a sense of humor and an appreciation of irony? Why else would She have arranged for the Saturday before Election Day 2020 to be Halloween? Of all elections, why this one?

It was a warm, sunny day in Costa Mesa, California. The candidate had returned home for one final opportunity to share her vision for Amberica in a place she knew would get it. She hoped and prayed it wasn't the only such place out of the hundreds she'd visited over the past sixteen months.

The venue for her appearance had been changed at the last minute when the facilities supervisor had called to notify her campaign manager that there'd been a terrible mixup in the scheduling. The indoor arena had already been booked, and no, they could not change it. So sorry. The campaign manager ranted and raved but with no results except to become increasingly upset.

"Have you tried the Pacific Amphitheatre?" the woman on the other end of the line had asked. "They may be able to accommodate you."

"How many will it seat?" the fuming manager asked.

"Oh, supposedly around eight thousand, but you might get them to open up the hillside, in which case you're probably talking about something like eighteen thousand."

"But we're expecting closer to thirty thousand."

"Yeah, well, you might ask some of them to stay home," the woman had replied, then hung up.

So, there we were on Halloween afternoon with a still irate campaign manager, a candidate who was far calmer than she had any right to be, and me sweating through my shirt and jacket, wishing I had a drink to fortify my nerves. And suddenly, it was time to go on. Our little clan of family and supporters came together for one last group hug, then we walked on stage to be greeted by an over capacity crowd who cheered uproariously and waved their banners and signs in the air.

As their candidate walked out, the cheering turned into laughter as they recognized that she was dressed in a deep purple witch's outfit, complete with pointed hat, and absolutely no make-up of any kind. The order had gone out from the Secret Service that masks of any type were banned, including any facial makeup.

The candidate stood before the adoring crowd of well wishers, waving and smiling for several minutes as the cheering continued. Finally, the crowd settled down enough for her to speak.

"I've been called many things during this campaign, including a witch and a bitch, so I figured it was time for me to embrace them both."

The crowd roared and cheered for another few minutes. And that's when it happened. One lone crack. I watched the candidate stumble back, as if in slow motion, momentarily losing her balance. I saw her campaign manager, dressed in one of her husband's football jerseys with his number 31 on the front and back, step in front to catch her, then heard two more rifle cracks ring out. I saw two crimson circles, one in the center of the 3 and the second a few inches to its right, blossom on this lovely lady's body as both women fell into a heap of humanity. Several people screamed and I heard a man's voice yell, "The candidate has been shot!", and then realized it was me yelling. Pandemonium broke out as people realized what had happened and they began to run, some towards the stage, many more away.

I remember that day as clearly as though it were yesterday, not years ago, for I stood on that platform. While I've done many things in my life of which I am not proud, I can say I stood my ground on that fateful day that changed the course of history for this country of Amberica forever. I even played a small role in helping the authorities locate the shooter by pointing to the glint of sunlight from the scope of the rifle. This is my account of everything that led up to that day when it looked like, for one excruciating moment, fear and hate had won over love.

It Starts

WILL SOMEONE WITH SOME smarts buy the Fake News and failing New York Times and either run it right or shut it down? Tweet by President Oscar Wellian

---

"WHAT? ARE YOU KIDDING me?" I asked as I put down my coffee mug and picked up the sheet of paper outlining possible topics to cover in the next twenty-four hours. "Another Democratic candidate running for president? How many does that make?"

"It's twenty-five by my count," Cynthia, my all too perky for a Monday morning assistant replied. "Take a closer look."

I did as instructed and read on. "Angeline Tarkington?" I asked, realizing I'm filled with nothing but questions this morning. "Really? I thought she had died."

"No, pretty sure she's alive," Cynthia replied. "If she's dead this is a much bigger story than first reported. Take a look at this editorial written in the *New York Times* this morning." She tossed a copy of the paper on my desk almost knocking over my cup of coffee.

"Hey watch it. Don't mess with my java ." I snatched up the paper and read the headline:

Angeline Tarkington Knows How to Defeat President Wellian

"What? You're not serious! Is this an infomercial?" I read to the bottom and recognized the byline. No, it was legit. I read it again more carefully. "Are you kidding me?"

Little did I know at the time how often I would end up asking that rhetorical question over the next sixteen months. Some entrepreneurial kid eventually put it on a T-shirt and sold thousands of them. Then the Angeline Tarkington campaign picked it up and sold millions. Long before the T-shirts appeared, I

started using it as my sign-off followed with " Watch this space," which I borrowed from my good friend and colleague, Roberta Meadows, who claims I
stole it not borrowed it. That part never made it to the T-shirt even though
Roberto privately threatened to sue me for copyright infringement. Yep, those
were the days when two old friends could kid around like that...before the shit
hit the fan.

But I'm getting ahead of myself. That was the first I heard that Angeline
Tarkington had joined the other two dozen candidates to run against President
Oscar Wellian, but that wasn't the first time our paths had crossed. A few days
after the *New York Times* piece caused enough of a ping to show up on my cynical radar screen, I remembered I had interviewed her during the early days of
my journalism career. I had even sold a Q&A article to a regional magazine, *The
Sun & Moon*. Someone at MSNBC saw it, loved it, and hired me.

Okay, that last statement isn't true. MSNBC didn't even exist back then
and wouldn't for another ten years. By then, I'd moved on from scrounging
around as a freelancer selling whatever I could to put food on the table to working for the *Washington Post* and later the very same *New York Times* which is
why I knew the editorial was legit. Melissa Guffy, who wrote the piece, had
been one of the women I'd slept with when Dottie and I went through one of
our rough periods. While she wasn't all that good in the sack, she knew how to
write a kickass editorial. Sorry, I digress again.

I wasn't at *The Times* very long before the new fledgling cable news channel
came calling. They had noticed that, not only could I connect words into in-
telligible sentences and passable paragraphs, but I also wasn't as much of an
introvert as most other writers. In fact, I had a loud mouth and, in my finer
moments, managed to speak truth to power. The execs at MSNBC didn't care
about that latter point, but they loved the idea of a loudmouth political pundit
heading up one of their talk shows.

So, they hired me. Over the next fifteen years, they moved me from one
time slot to another. Those were the days when I was part of a dedicated and
committed journalistic team where integrity mattered. I collected a lot of favors by never refusing an assignment and filling in whenever someone needed
their slot covered.

I will not lie. It was tough, tough on me and even tougher on my marriage.
After all that hard work and dedication the SOB exec who hired me eventually

fired me. The network told the public I was on an extended leave of absence for health reasons, and that was partly true. I spent a luxurious six weeks in a private and exclusive rehab center drying out. Unfortunately, the rehab didn't stick, but at least it lasted long enough for me to talk another of the execs into giving me back my show. During my stay in rehab, I collected a lot of great one-liners which I started sprinkling into my shows and my ratings slowly came back to an acceptable level, and I learned a lot from my time in rehab. Most importantly, I learned to keep my excess drinking private and mostly on the weekends.

A COUPLE OF WEEKS AFTER Angeline Tarkington entered the race and the *New York Times* editorial made a splash, Angeline's name came up again. Well, it wasn't really Angeline who I became aware of first, but her buxom campaign manager. My god, what a figure! The thing that caught my attention most, besides her gorgeous breasts, was what a smart and savvy political operative she was. She knew how to use all her tools and talents to benefit her candidate of choice.

I was standing in the newsroom discussing with Edward Stenson, my producer, which of the twenty-five candidates we should invite on the show next, when I glanced up to see this stately blonde, wearing a brilliant emerald green dress, fixing to leave. I leaned over closer to Ed, who hardly came up to my shoulder and was almost as wide as he was tall.

"Who the hell is that?" I asked, nodding in the woman's direction.

"Oh, that's Stella Romaine, Angeline Tarkington's campaign manager. Quite a looker, isn't she?"

"I'll say," I replied, trying unsuccessfully to take my eyes off her and place them back on the desk full of the candidates' pictures. "Angeline Tarkington? She's the self-help author that announced she was running a couple weeks ago, right?"

"Yep, that's the one." Edward tapped one of the photos—an attractive woman who looked to be in her late forties, though I found out later she was just about to celebrate her fifty-ninth birthday. "That's her. We have her tagged simply as 'Author.' We weren't sure what else to use. She's kind of a New Age

evangelist, though she specifically asked that we not use 'New Age' or 'evangelist.' So, it's 'Author' for now." He tossed her photo to one side and picked up
the photo of a gray-haired man who had already started making the rounds on
the talk show circuit.

"I think we better go ahead and book Senator O'Hare if we can get him.
What do you say?"

I shook my head and retrieved Angeline's photo from the pile. "No, let's
color outside the lines on this one. How about giving her office a call? On second thought, never mind. I'll take care of the matter myself." Still holding Angeline's picture in my hand, I walked over to Stella and introduced myself.

Note to Reader: So, my question to you is this. Was that my well-honed
journalistic instincts guiding me to the story of the century? Of course not.
What led to Angeline's and my paths crossing again came from much lower in
my anatomy. Told you God has a sense of humor.

Making a Move - Bad Idea

THE FAKE NEWS MEDIA is insane with their conspiracy theories and blind hatred. @MSNBC is the worst by far, and don't get me started with that idiot, Gramarly. Tweet by President Oscar Wellian

"HELLO, I'M BRASTEN Gramarly," I said, holding my hand out to Stella while making sure she could see the photo of Angeline I held in my other hand.

"A pleasure to meet you, Mr. Gramarly," Stella replied, taking my hand and holding it firmly in her own. Did I feel a burst of sexual energy between us in that moment our hands touched? I surely did, and I had no doubt she did as well. "I know who you are. You're on my list of people to meet today, so thanks for helping me check off one more item on my list."

"Are you a list-maker too?" I asked, continuing to hold her hand despite feeling her effort to reclaim it. Finally, I reluctantly let go.

"Oh, yes, for sure. I'll even add an item I've done that wasn't on the list just so I can check it off," Stella continued, smiling warmly. "We must always be on the lookout for the simple joys of life, and checking off items on my list is certainly one of them."

I chuckled. "So true, so true." *Like the simple joys of holding a beautiful woman's hand as well,* I started to say, but then heard one of Dottie's familiar groans from the ethers, and just managed to keep my trap shut. *Be professional...for once in your life.*

Okay, okay. I'll do my best. Get off my case.

"Pardon me?" Stella asked with a perplexed look on her Helen-of-Troy face. "What case are you referring to?"

Now it was my turn to groan, realizing I'd spoken that last comment out loud.

"Oh, no...nothing," I stammered, now flustered by my ineptness. I held up the photo. "I believe this is who you came to see me about?"

"Yes, exactly. I so love a man who gets right to the point," Stella replied.

Great, how about drinks with me tonight after work? It was at that moment that I noticed the wedding ring on her left hand. *Damn! Already taken. But when had that ever stopped me? I mean, a little innocent flirting...no one would mind that, right?*

Not in this day and age with sexual harassment in the workplace being so rampant, came Dottie's unsolicited response. *Keep it professional.*

"I was hoping we might look at some dates in the not too distant future when Ms. Tarkington could..."

"How about this Friday?" I asked. *Afterwards, maybe we could fit in those drinks and see what develops from there.* But I knew better than to say anything. I could feel Dottie breathing down my neck from where her tiny form sat on my right shoulder, and see Cynthia, my assistant, leaning in our direction from across the room listening in on our conversation.

"You really are a man of action," Stella replied. "I'll need to check Ms. Tarkington's schedule, but unless she has a meeting with President Wellian himself, I'm sure we can make that work." She reached out with her soft, supple hand and shook mine. She turned to leave.

If I'd been smart and listened to my moral compass, Dottie, I would have left it there, but it was that final handshake that did me in. I imagined how soft the rest of her body would feel under mine, and well...I went for it.

"Listen, before you go..." She turned back to me, and I caught a whiff of the most alluring perfume I'd ever smelled. "How about meeting me after work today for drinks, and dinner, and..." I left the question hanging expectantly.

Her smile disappeared, being immediately replaced with a stern edginess. She held up her hand with the wedding ring on it. "That, Mr. Gramarly, is out of the question. I am happily married."

"Well, I won't tell him if you don't," I bulled ahead, my tongue clearly being directed by something other than my rational mind.

She chuckled, but it was empty of any humor. "Do you have any idea who my husband is?"

Why would I care? I thought. *It's you who I want to sleep with. I'm not into three-ways, at least not with another man involved.* I shook my head.

"Google him," she said, then turned on her heels and started walking off. "And the interview is still on for Friday, right?"

"Huh, sure, I guess," I replied as I watched her stroll away, an aching of longing in my heart...well a good bit lower than that if I tell the truth, which I've promised to do. *Way to be professional,* Dottie said. *Like a professional gigolo.*

I cringed, but the condemnation was far from over. Cynthia walked by with a smile that reminded me of the old cartoons where Sylvester cat has just eaten Tweety Bird. "You know, boss, deep down inside, I know you're a good person. Look at all the times you've stepped in and covered for other hosts, worked overtime when needed. Really good. But I tell you, when it comes to women, you're clueless and crass. And if you aren't careful, your penis is going to lead you straight to a sexual harassment lawsuit. Mark my words."

As she started to walk away, I asked, "Well, who is her husband, anyway?"

"Dallas Romaine, star running back for the Washington Redskins," she said over her shoulder, then turned to add, "Program has him listed at six foot three and two hundred twenty pounds. He'll snap you in half like a toothpick if he finds out you hit on his wife. I hope I'm there to watch."

UNFORTUNATELY, AT THAT point my male ego went to work, and between Monday and Friday it had plenty of opportunities to twist and turn what had happened or not happened between Stella and me. I'm sure some psychologist would be quick to point out all the times I'd been rejected by the opposite sex, including and particularly my mother. All of those times were in play again. Why? Because I never resolved those issues, and never asked forgiveness. So says my imaginary psychologist, who happens to bear a striking resemblance to Dottie. Grrr!

In any case, by Friday's showtime, I was ready to go hunt some bear. My plan was simple. Stella was Angeline Tarkington's campaign manager. Stella had rejected my innocent invitation to drinks and dinner, so I was obligated to utterly destroy Ms. Tarkington and to reveal her for the New Age fake that she no doubt was. I mean, isn't it up to each of us to keep the Universe's balance in check? Even Angeline Tarkington would agree with me on that.

So, I had a simple plan, created over several days by a top strategist and an amazing talk show host. Hell, by the time the show started, I'd convinced myself that I was doing my patriotic duty by uncovering the shyster. Oh, how the best laid plans of mice and men...you know the rest.

I zipped through the first segments of the show with ease. At each commercial break, I pulled out my list of questions with which I planned to nail Angeline to the wall. I continued to tinker with the wording and order, feeling increasingly good about the design and justified in my actions. Reject me, will you? Not without paying dearly for it.

The plan started to unfold right on cue with the tagline underneath Angeline's name. Instead of "Author", I'd had the graphic team insert "New Age Guru," and I made sure Angeline saw it as she took her seat. But it didn't seem to phase her.

So, we have a cool one here, I thought. *Let's see how long that lasts.*

"Alright, we're back with my last guest for the evening, who happens to also be the last person to throw her name in the pot to become our next President of the United States. Welcome to the show, Angeline Tarkington."

She opened her mouth to respond but I never gave her a chance. "Let's jump right in. Tell me, why would a New Age guru like yourself decide at the last minute to do such a crazy thing as try to run for President of the United States?"

She closed her mouth and smiled. *Boy, do I have her with that one. There's no way to win by answering that question,* I thought, and, not for the last time that night, was I ever wrong.

"What a great question," Angeline replied. "Let's see, you've managed to weave in 'New Age guru' right from the start." She pointed behind her at the screen. "You also have characterized my actions as both crazy and last minute, suggesting I do things impulsively and without much thought. Kinda like an airhead, wouldn't you say? Or some wackadoodle. I believe that was the term *The Washington Post* recently coined."

I opened my mouth to reply, but this time Angeline continued right on. "But disregarding all those derogatory remarks intended to raise the ratings of your show, it really is a good question. Why did I choose to run for the highest office of these United States of Amberica? It's because, like so many of my fellow Ambericans, I'm concerned about the direction our current President

Wellian is leading us. And, like my fellow Ambericans, when I took the time to pray to God as to what I could do with the gifts and talents He has so graciously bestowed on me, the answer came back clear as a bell. "Run...run, Angeline, run." She smiled, first at me, and then straight into the camera. "So, here I am everyone. I'm Angeline Tarkington, not a New Age guru, but just a concerned citizen like you, and I'm running to be your President. Next question."

And it went downhill from there. I don't know what happened. I even went back and watched the tape several times, and I still don't know for sure. I think her first reply was so right on, first about what I had done to undermine her from the start, and then to so adroitly turn my piece of shit question into gold with such an authentic answer, I just lost it. After that, every question seemed so trivial and off purpose and offputting because they were, so I started to wing it, and in this case, winging it sounded like me babbling almost incoherently. Thankfully, my producer saved me with a stern message in my headset. "Go to commercial—NOW!"

So, we did. And for the first time in a very long time, I did not close out my own show. I failed to even say, "Are you kidding me? Watch this space, and goodnight." No, the network sent the viewers straight to the next show because I was in the men's room puking.

Late Evening

WOW, MATTHEW HIGGINS was just fired from ABC for "inappropriate sexual behavior in the workplace." But when will the top executives at MSNBC & CNN be fired for all their fake news? Tweet by President Oscar Wellian

LATER THAT EVENING I sat in my plush New York apartment a couple blocks from the studio and nursed my third Old Fashioned. As was customary, I took this time to debrief and drink, and if I didn't pass out, begin to plan the next week. I watched the show I'd just completed a second time, cringing when I got to the Angeline Tarkington interview. *Hmm,* I thought, *cringing seems to becoming a habit. I mustn't continue doing it. My neck is becoming so stiff, I'll have to make an appointment with my chiropractor. Or better yet, with Mitzy,* the lovely masseuse that Edward had recently turned me on to.

"*There you go again, thinking with your penis,*" Dottie said from across the room.

I groaned. "What are you doing here?"

"*Why, it's Friday night and you're drunk as a skunk. Where else would I be?*" she replied as she walked over and sat down on the arm of my overstuffed chair. "*Feeling sorry for yourself, again?*"

I nodded. No need to try to hide it from my wife. She could read me like a book, always had. "Did you see the show?" I asked.

She nodded. "*Yep, she really ate you for lunch, and well deserved, I might add.*"

"Hey, who's side are you on?"

"*On the side of Truth, Justice and the American Way,*" she quipped. "*In other words, on her side in this case.*"

"You women always stick together."

"Can you blame us, given how patriarchal the world still is, though that is changing, and I've a feeling Angeline Tarkington may play a significant role in that transformation, among others. Which is part of the reason you feel so threatened."

"I do not," I started to say, but then knew better. Like a book she reads me. I shrugged instead. "So, how do you know so much about Tarkington? Don't tell me you're one of her New Age fans."

"I read a few of her books in my day," Dottie replied. *"I found them well thought out and written by an intelligent woman with a good head on her shoulders. I also read the article you wrote, plus, if you recall, you had me transcribe the lengthy interview you had with her."*

"Oh, yeah, that's right. Wonder whatever happened to those notes?"

Dottie pointed across the room to my laptop and then faded away. Clearly, her purpose for tonight's visit was complete.

I slowly rose from my chair and weaved my way over to the computer and spent the next couple of hours first searching through my files, then reading the notes and the final Q&A piece. As I finally finished around 3 AM, I sat back in my chair. The ice from my fifth Old Fashioned was all but gone. "Okay, so she's not some New Age wackadoodle. Then, who the hell is she?" I vowed to find out come Monday morning.

IT TURNED OUT TO BE the weekend from hell. I managed to sleep late, as I usually did on Saturdays, good show or bad, and as I customarily do, I zipped over to my Facebook and Twitter accounts while munching on a slice of dry toast washed down with a mug of bulletproof coffee, which I found helped with the hangover.

What didn't help was what I found on social media. Even for a weekend, I was shocked how many people were posting and tweeting about how Angeline Tarkington had taken me to the cleaners on my own show. Headlines like:

Has B Gramarly Met his Match? and

A. Tarkington Pulls a Gramarly on the Old (and soon to retire) Master

Soon to retire? Who says? Well, several hundred retweets suggested many thought it was a good idea. I slammed the phone down and went to take a leak, but of course, I couldn't let it go. Within minutes I was checking the feed again for more self abuse. Then the thought came to me—a thought I very rarely have. What would this do for the show's ratings?

What? Now I was channeling Edward, my producer. Who the fuck cares about the ratings? My job was secure, or was it? I surfed over to Edward's Twitter account to see if he'd posted anything, but of course, he hadn't. He almost never did. He left that to Cynthia and some of our other assistants, usually after the tweets had been approved from upstairs.

Finally, in frustration, I turned the phone off, grabbed the leash, and took Rufus, my Blue Tick Coonhound, for a stroll in the park. He was very grateful, having needed to keep his legs crossed to not pee on the carpet.

"Yeah, well, at least you need me, boy," I said, as I watched him lift his leg and whiz on a bush, a relieved expression on his face. "I can just see us now. You and me on some street corner in a week or two with a tin cup and a sign, *Will lie and cheat for food*, or something like that." He looked up at me and farted. Everyone's a critic these days.

I managed to stay away from social media for the rest of the weekend, which meant turning off all the customary notifications. Instead, I busied myself planning the next week's show schedule, at least the topics and interviews I'd recommend to Edward on Monday morning. *Assuming I still have a job*, I heard myself say, and just barely resisted cringing over the thought. After all, I'm beyond middle-age and the thought of being back out on the job market was almost as frightening as being back on the meat market of dating. At least there, I had a choice whether to play or not, which for the most part I didn't. I could live without the hassles of a relationship, but no job? That was a different story. I had certain habits and addictions like eating and drinking that required a certain level of consistent income.

You'll be fine, I told myself. *After all, it was just one interview, and it wasn't all that bad.* See, I'm good at lying even to myself.

By Monday morning, I was back in the saddle with a game plan and everything. I walked into the morning meeting with clear purpose.

"I want to schedule Angeline Tarkington back on my show ASAP," I said boldly, without so much as a good morning.

Edward looked up from his copy of the *New York Times* and smiled. "If I'm not mistaken, isn't that the same woman that handed you your testicles on a platter Friday night?"

I shrugged. Well, it's better than cringing, isn't it? "It wasn't that bad," I replied.

"No?" He flipped the newspaper open to the Op-ed section. "Seems the *New York Times* doesn't agree."

This time I did cringe as I read the headline:

Newest Dem Candidate Shows Up Gramarly

"Listen," Edward went on. "Why would you want a repeat match after being KO'ed in the first round?"

I hated how Edward could always find some sports metaphor to make his point, but this time I thought I'd run with it if it meant I'd get my way.

"Exactly, a 'Rematch of the Century', like Sonny Liston and..." Me, I'm not nearly as good at the metaphors, not being all that big a sports fan. "Well, you know what I mean," I forged on. "You get me the 'rematch' and I promise the ratings will skyrocket."

Suddenly, Edward showed some sign of interest. I probably would have been fine to just keep my mouth shut at that point and let him make the decision, but hey, I'm Brasten Gramarly, who never seems to learn when to shut his mouth.

"In fact, if we don't have a ten point uptick, you'll have my resignation on your desk the following day."

He stuck his hand out and we shook on it. As I walked off, the litany began: *I'm really screwed this time, yes I am, yes I am.*

Interview #2

OUR FOREIGN ENEMIES are drooling over the small chance that one of the Democrat Candidates might unseat me. Will never happen. Tweet by President Oscar Wellian

ON A STIFLING FRIDAY night, I sat in the chair as Mindy, the makeup artist, tried to take ten years off my face while Cynthia fanned me with a magazine in an effort to keep the makeup from running down into my shoes. Earlier in the week I had asked her to stay late on Friday night and make sure to keep me positive.

"You're kidding, right? Is this one of your silly jokes about me being too upbeat and perky?"

"No, no, not at all," I replied, now regretting all those jabs even though I really did find her too energetic especially on Monday mornings. "No, I have a big interview with Angeline Tarkington and..."

"Yeah, I heard about that. You really are crazy, aren't you? A ten point upturn in the rating over one show. What were you on when you made that bet?"

I shrugged. "I like living on the edge sometimes. It helps keep me sharp, which is also why I need you there to keep me out of my head. You know, be my cheerleader of sorts?"

Cynthia stared at me for a long moment with a look of suspicion on her face. Finally, she asked, "And what's in it for me?"

That's my girl. I'd taught her well. I felt a wave of pride as I pretended to ponder the question, even though I was prepared to respond. "Time and a half for the hours after 5 PM."

Cynthia shook her head. "I already get that from the network. No, what are *you* prepared to give me to spice up the deal a bit more?"

I resisted reaching out to hug here, my pride was so great. Instead, I replied, "Okay, all that plus a two-fifty bonus under the table so you don't have to report it on your taxes. Deal?"

"Deal!" She replied, dancing around. "There's a Louis Vuitton handbag I want and that should just about give me enough."

"Really, how nice," I replied. Of course I knew all about the handbag, having seen the ad for it sitting on her desk.

So, here we were, Mindy, Cynthia, and me preparing for the 'fight of the century,' and no lie, I was nervous. What if I blew this one again? Would Edward really hold me to my promise? I'd just as soon not find out.

"Fan harder," I ordered and Cynthia responded.

"We had such a positive response last week from our next guest's appearance, that we moved heaven and earth to have her back on the show, so welcome Angeline Tarkington to our show again." This time I shut up and let her respond. Already an improvement, right?

"Thank you, Brasten, for inviting me back."

"I understand that in another interview you're quoted as having referred to the 'the darker psychic forces at work in our country.' Would you care to expand on that comment?"

"Certainly," Angeline replied. She leaned forward for emphasis. "Our current president is fostering a deep part of our country's collective consciousness, the darker side of fear and hate. It's time for us to bring that phase to an end and replace it with a more caring and compassionate consciousness, one of Universal Love, brother and sisterhood."

Good answer, I thought, but hardly one that will spike the ratings, so I decided I needed to go in deeper and see what gold I could mine. "I understand that you are a minister, is that correct?"

"I led a church for a time, though I'm not ordained," Angeline replied.

"A Unity Church, if I'm not mistaken," I countered pretending innocence.

"Well, we prefer calling them Unity Centers but yes, that's correct."

"Some say that Unity is a religious cult so would that make you a cult leader?"

Angeline sat there and blinked several times before replying. "I'm not sure to whom you are referring when you say 'some' but I would reply that they are misinformed. Unity is a Christian based organization who believes in the authentic spiritual inquiry of all religions and faiths."

Darn, another perfectly acceptable answer, I thought. *Oh well, on to the next question.*

"Let's take a few minutes to look at some of the policies and plans you advocate, like a Department of Peace and another one, Department for Children..."

"Yes, that's correct," Tarkington replied. "If we truly want peace and I believe all Americans do, we should devote as much time and money to fostering it as we do in preparing for war. I'm in favor of giving our military everything that they indicate that they need, but our government has bowed to the demands of the military-industrial complex and our budget reflects this."

She paused to take a sip of water, and then was at it again. "As for my proposed Department for Children, for far too long we've given lip service to our children, claiming they are the future of our country, but then not delivering on what they truly need for that future to be bright. So, yes, that's one very important part of my platform."

The interview continued like that for several more minutes.

"I'm curious, and I imagine many of our viewers are as well, what made you decide to run for President? I mean, you've had a very successful career as an author and speaker. Why jump into the political arena, especially one that by your own admission is so broken and dysfunctional?"

Angeline gazed at me for several seconds with a serene look on her face. In that moment, she really did look the part of an angel. Finally, she replied, "It was a couple of years ago. I was in New York for a number of speaking engagements and book signings for my new book. It was a hectic schedule to say the least, but in the midst of it, I slipped away early one morning to visit the Statue of Liberty. As many times as I'd been in New York, I'd never taken the time to visit it. While I was there, I read the passage inscribed on it. The first line really spoke to me, almost like Lady Liberty was whispering the words in my ears. 'Give me your tired, your poor, your huddled masses yearning to breathe free.'"

I realized she and I had much in common. I had been working tirelessly for decades for the 'huddled masses yearning to breathe free.' That's when I realized she was inviting me to play a bigger game. It simply took me a bit to realize what form that would take."

Angeline smiled at me. "Thank you for the question."

And just like that, it was time to thank Angeline for appearing on the show and to sign off.

"So, that's another week in the madcap world of news and politics. Are you kidding me? Watch this space. Until next week, this is Brasten Gramarly, good night."

I waited for the light on the camera to wink off before turning back to Angeline. "Well, that wasn't so bad, was it?"

"No, it was fine. By comparison to last week, you were quite professional, all things considered." She smiled and reached out to grasp my hands before asking, "How is your wife?"

"What?" I said, taken aback by the personal question. "Why, she's dead. She died over two years ago."

Instead of an "Oh, I'm sorry to hear that. I didn't know," Angeline leaned in closer and strengthened her grip on my hands. "Yes, I know. How is she?"

I opened my mouth to reply even though I really didn't know how to answer her question, but before I could do so, Cynthia was at my elbow saying, "Edward would like to see you in his office right away."

I nodded to her and looked back at Angeline who just smiled again and patted my hand. "You have a good weekend. I'm sure Edward won't hold you to your promise. It was made in a moment of desperation and fear. There's a lot of that going around these days. Good night."

Turns out she was right. The show did all right with a rating increase of about five points, only half way to what I'd promised, but Edward was pleased that I'd not made a fool of myself, even though he did harangue on me a bit about the Unity question. But overall he was satisfied, and I still had my job, as well as a new level of intrigue about Angeline Tarkington. What had she meant by that question about Dottie, and how in the hell did she know about my promise to Edward? So far, I had far more questions than answers.

A Troubled Night

Our country must have strong borders and extreme vetting—NOW! We need vetting all over Europe and, indeed, the world. What a terrible mess! Tweet by President Oscar Wellian

I WATCHED RERUNS OF *Friday Night Lights* as I sipped on my Old Fashioned, hoping to pick up some sports metaphors I could lay on Edward come Monday morning. I wasn't ready to check social media just yet. Besides, what did it matter what all those clowns said? Edward said he was satisfied with the show and released me from my promise...just as Angeline had said he would. I paused the show and fixed myself another drink while thinking about that last conversation. What the hell had the woman meant by asking me about my dead wife, anyway?

"*You could have asked her to elaborate on the question,*" the comment came from behind me where Dottie stood leaning against the dining room table. "*After all, you are a journalist, of sorts. Questions are one of your most effective tools, at least that's what you used to tell me.*"

I glanced at the bottle of Maker's Mark trying to remember whether this was my third or fourth drink. "You're early tonight," I observed.

She shrugged and strolled over to the couch where she stretched out and smiled. "*I heard you call my name,*" she replied.

I started to argue the point, then thought better of it.

"*So, why didn't you ask her?*" Dottie persisted.

"I guess I didn't really want to know," I replied truthfully. "Besides, what business is it of hers how you and I are getting along?"

"*That's not actually what she asked.*"

"Well, all right. How are you, so next time she asks, I can answer her truthfully."

"Mostly curious these days," Dottie replied.

"Curious about what?" But even as I asked it, I knew I wasn't going to like the answer.

"I'm curious why you're giving this woman such a hard time." Dottie sat up and glared at me.

"What do you mean? I'm giving her air time, which, if I'm not mistaken, is more vital to a candidate than virtually anything else, including real air."

She nodded and pursed her lips, her sign that she was considering my reply.

"Fair enough, you are doing that, but let me ask you another question. What if this woman is for real? Why don't you start listening, really listening to what she has to say rather than working so hard to bring her down to your level?"

"That's two questions," I replied in an effort to avoid answering either one. When Dottie continued sitting there waiting me out, I finally replied. "I don't know. I'm just not convinced she is for real."

"And how might you find out?"

I looked down and dropped a couple of ice cubes in my drink, and then, there it was, like a lightbulb glowing over my head. "I'd get my research team to vet her!" I looked up to thank Dottie but she was no longer there.

I took a couple swallows of my drink, then pulled out my cellphone. I waited as the phone rang several times at the other end. "Hello," a sleepy voice finally answered.

"Olivia, this is Brasten. I need for you to call the team together. I need you to thoroughly vet Angeline Tarkington."

"Brasten? Are you kidding me?"

"Yes, that Brasten."

"No, really, are you kidding me? It's 3 AM. Couldn't this wait until morning, or better yet, Monday?"

"No, it can't wait. This woman is running for president. We need to find out if she's real or not."

"Real? What in the world...never mind. I'll get on it. Now put away the booze and get some sleep." Click.

I looked at the phone for a moment, smiling. Sleep? Not now, I was too energized for sleep. No, it was time for a visit to *The Dive.*

I'M NOT SURE WHAT HAD first attracted me to *The Dive* all those years ago. Probably the fact that I could drink 'out in public' without being accosted by fans or irate right wingers. Whatever it was, it had become my place, and though I didn't visit it that often, I knew I could count on it to be there when I needed it and that it would be virtually unchanged.

It's still a mystery to me how the place has managed to survive all these years as the nearby stores and restaurants slowly transformed the area to a fairly high class and expensive location, but Lulu, the owner and frequent bartender, had managed to keep its doors open without putting one cent into renovations or even new paint as far as I could tell. Like I said, the atmosphere of *The Dive* was one of the truly consistent aspects of my life.

And it truly was a dive, just as the name implied. It wasn't just that you had to descend down a flight of stairs to get to it. You had to clomp down two flights into the sub-basement area of a high end apartment building. That's probably why it had managed to survive so long. Everyone but its most loyal customers must have forgotten it was there.

The loyal customers, of which I was one, were another draw. I could count on there being no more than a dozen patrons there on any given night—committed drinkers who wanted to rub elbows with others of like kind without a lot of meaningless chit chat.

So, there I was, walking down the rickety stairs a little after 3 AM, and as expected, there was Lulu, drying glasses with a towel that looked more like a rag that had come with the place. I stood in the doorway for a moment waiting for my eyes to adjust to the dim lighting and counting the numbers of people at the bar and tables. An even dozen counting me. All was right with the world. I stepped in and nodded to Lulu, who nodded back to me. No needs for words. We had our own form of communication mostly composed of body movements, hand signals and a few grunts here and there. Yes, *The Dive* is my little paradise away from home. I have simple tastes except for when it comes to my booze. Where I drink it, *The Dive* fits my needs perfectly.

Debate #1

I PREDICT VERY LOW ratings for the Democratic Debate tonight. No one cares to watch if I'm not there. Tweet by President Oscar Wellian

IT WAS ANOTHER "ARE you kidding me?" moment the morning I received word that Angeline Tarkington would be on stage for the first debate, having just barely qualified at the last minute, despite the fact that most of the mainstream media was either ignoring her or berating her for her 'wackadoodle' ideas. However, a little research revealed that she had a significant following of enthusiastic fans who weighed in heavily for her on social media and by contributing a dollar or more to her campaign fund.

I'd had more than one sleepless night trying to figure out what her intention had been when she'd asked me how my deceased wife was doing, so as the debate night rolled around, I came up with a game plan to balance the scale just a bit.

While our network would be the host for the first debate, I had conveniently not been included in the panel of moderators, but that didn't stop me. Actually, it played right into my plan. No one could point the finger at me for what was to happen. I would implement my plan through a surrogate, Roberta Meadows. Over the years, I'd accumulated close to a dozen 'favor chips', mostly from sitting in for Roberta when she had to get away to recharge, so I figured it was high time to call in a few. On the day before the debate, I met her in her office and handed her a small slip of paper.

"What's this?" she asked, staring at the folded paper with the same look of curiosity with which she approached all her assignments.

"Open it," I instructed, and as she did so, I continued. "It's a question I want you to ask Angeline Tarkington tomorrow night."

Even before she read it, Roberta shook her head. "You know questions are thoroughly discussed by the committee before they make it on the list." She unfolded the paper anyway and read it.

"Are you kidding me?" she asked, continuing to shake her head.

"That's my line, remember? And no, I'm not kidding. It's worth a favor chip if you slip it in sometime while the debate is on air."

"No, no way," Roberta replied, dropping the paper on her desk. *That's a good sign,* I thought. *She didn't throw it back at me or drop it in the wastebasket, so clearly the negotiations are on.*

"Ahh, come on, be a sport," I continued, reaching down and nudging the paper closer to her. "Okay, two favor chips. Just ask the question, and you'll be that much closer to us being even."

"Not all that close," Roberta replied, but as she did so, she continued to stare at the paper. "Why would you want to ask such a question anyway? Are you trying to ruin this woman's political career before it gets off the ground?"

"What's going on between Tarkington and me is my business. I just need you to ask that one simple question, and when you do...," I paused for emphasis, "...I'll redeem three favor chips. Just think how many hours I worked to cover your slots so you could go deep sea fishing."

She continued to stare at the slip of paper before finally picking it up and reading it again. "Well, I might be able to figure some way to ask the question without being laughed off the stage. Let me think about it and get back to you."

I nodded and tried not to smile too broadly, but I knew I had her, and the best part was that I'd been ready to offer as much as five favors. Receiving an almost certain yes for just three was a bargain. So, feeling magnanimous, I offered to take Roberta to lunch. I figured it wouldn't hurt to sweeten the pot just a bit, but she declined.

"Last time I joined you for one of your 'liquid lunches', I had a splitting headache the rest of the day. No, I've got too much work to do. I'll let you know my final answer before I step on stage tomorrow night. You going to be there?"

"Sure thing. I wouldn't miss it for the world." I turned around and left her office. I had pretty much given up drinking during lunch, but today I felt like I deserved to give myself a treat. A couple dry martinis might just do the trick. When I returned from lunch, my slip of paper lay on my desk. I picked it and read Roberta's scrawling handwriting.

I accept.

I fist pumped the air. Game on!

———✝✝✝✝✝———

THE ALMOST CAPACITY crowd was buzzing as I arrived on the set the night of the first debate a good hour before show time. *Wow,* I thought. *Edward and Arnie must be already patting themselves on the back with this kind of turnout.* Edward worked closely with Arnie, one of the uppity ups at the network, who had a reputation for running a tight ship. As far as I was concerned, he was a tight ass that didn't know how to keep his nose out of my business. A good crowd at a debate almost always meant a good viewing crowd as well. With this many people already in their seats, clearly this would not be a night we'd have to go out on the street and pay people to come in and fill the empty spots. No, not on this night.

I walked around a bit, schmoozing with my colleagues and their support team. Everyone was in good spirits, anticipating a banner night for the network, but I didn't see Roberta until the last minute before she was due to step on stage with the other three moderators. From across the room, I gave her a warm smile and a thumbs up. She responded with a frown and a tentative wave of the hand. Clearly she was nervous over what was about to happen. I hoped she wouldn't forget the question or decide at the last minute to refrain from asking it. Suddenly, I was nervous as well.

The field of candidates had been decreased to twenty when five of them did not meet the criteria to qualify for the debate. Angeline had been the last one to make it. The field had then been divided into two nights through a random drawing, which resulted in all three front runners appearing the first night along with Angeline. *Another fortuitous event for her,* I thought, but then, as it turned out, maybe not, as the three primary candidates dominated the night, in part because they received the most questions from the moderators and because they were also deft at butting in for rebuttal. As I watched Angeline at the far end of the stage, she reminded me of a deer caught in the headlights of an oncoming car. *She's used to being on a stage with adoring fans out in the audience,* I thought, *not with nine other speakers all with more debate experience than her.*

Oh, my god, am I starting to feel sorry for her? Where has my journalistic unbiased position gone?

She did eventually get in a comment or two, and Morrie finally slipped her a bone of a question that she handled well, even though he cut her off in mid-sentence with a question to Senator O'hare. It looked like the night was not going to end well for Angeline at all, along with several others who'd received the short end of the debate stick. Then, I remembered the question I'd planted. Would Roberta go ahead and ask it? If so, it would need to be quick since the debate was winding up.

Morrie had just started his closing points and was getting ready to thank the candidates and the audience for a fine night with democracy well on display, when Roberta spoke up from his left.

"Before we end tonight, I have one last question I'd like to ask. This one is directed to you, Ms. Tarkington." Morrie frowned at her, but let her go on. "I know this may sound like an unusual question to ask on a political debate stage, but since you're becoming known as the spiritual candidate in many circles, I think you'll understand why I'm asking it."

Roberta paused for just a second as Angeline nodded and smiled, clearly pleased to finally be asked a question. Me? I groaned, already regretting my impulse to seek revenge once again. "Ms. Tarkington, do you believe in ghosts? You know, spirits who come back from the dead?"

Angeline paused and blinked several times before answering. "Yes, I see," she started, clearly uncertain how to proceed. She took a deep breath, then let it out. "It really is an excellent question, and I appreciate your asking it, for it gives me the opportunity to address beliefs in general. You see, in a democracy like ours, beliefs are an important part of our rights as human beings living in a free country. We have the right to believe what we choose, to practice or not practice the religion of our choice, and to allow those around us to do so as well. Our current administration doesn't support that level of democracy, but instead tries to force or manipulate us into believing what he believes, and he uses the powerful tools of fear and hate to accomplish this. A Tarkington administration will never use fear or hate to force the public into the darkness. I will always shine the light of Universal Love on not only the citizens of the United States, but also the world. Thank you for the question."

There was a moment of silence. Then, the crowd rose to its feet as one body and clapped and cheered, drowning out Morrie's sign off. The first debate was over, but its ramifications had just begun.

Wackadoodle or not, I'd never seen anyone who could turn a terrible question into pure gold. *I think we're in for a wild ride over the next few months,* I thought, as I went looking for Roberta to apologize.

Post Debate

WHAT'S UP WITH MSNBC wacko Roberta? Has she finally lost it? Her ratings are sure to drop like a rock. So deserving. Tweet by President Oscar Wellian

I FOUND HER IN THE Green Room taking a long drink from a flask she'd brought with her. Seeing me, I heard a low growl come from her and she held the flask up as though to throw it at my head, but then thought better of it. "You're too worthless to waste good booze on," she said, as she put the flask to her lips and took another swallow.

"Hey, we had a great night, all things considered. You were fantastic out there," I added with as much enthusiasm as I could muster, which only made it sound that much more inauthentic.

"Yeah, great, really great. I'm sure that's what Arnie wants to tell me as well, which is why he's ordered me to come to his office immediately." She glared at me a moment longer and shook her head. "Three measly favors. I should have held out for five. Hell, I could have asked for the whole slate to be clean and it still wouldn't have been payment enough. My integrity is worth more than anything you have." She took another pull on the flask before putting it away in her jacket pocket. "Do me a favor and never, ever do me a favor again."

With that, she stormed out of the room, leaving me alone with my thoughts. I knew she'd eventually cool down and probably forgive me. At least I hoped she would. She'd been a good friend through the years, and I really didn't have so many that I could afford to lose one over such a blunder.

I found out later that Roberta had taken the blame for the inappropriate question and didn't rat me out to Arnie, which just proved how much of a good friend she was. The news just made me feel that much worse. Dottie was right. I can be a real asshole when I want to be. In fact, lately it seemed to be my default move.

THE NEXT DAY THERE was an active Twitter Storm as social media speculated what was going on with MSNBC and one of their top show hosts, Roberta Meadows. Roberta refused to say a word to anyone, especially not to me. It was unlike her to hold a grudge, so I began to worry that I may have really wrecked a good friendship. To make matters worse, the way Angeline had responded to the question with poise and an insightful answer just made her the darling of the debate. So, no revenge for me either.

That afternoon I met with the head of my research team, Deanna Jacobs. "What have you found on this Tarkington woman?" I asked.

"You mean our next President of Amberica?" Deanna quipped back.

"Oh, don't tell me you've drunk the Kool-Aid as well."

She shrugged and smiled. "To answer your question, not much as this point, but we're still digging. She does seem to have quite a loyal following from her books and speaking tours."

"Yeah, yeah, I know all that," I replied petulantly. "But I want to know does she have any skeletons in her closet that we should know about. After all, like you alluded to, she could end up as our next president."

Deanna paused for a moment and bit her lower lip. I knew that sign meant she was thinking about something and whether to let me in on it or not. I waited, pretending patience that I didn't feel.

"Well," she finally replied. "We've not verified this yet...." She paused again, and I imagined reaching out and choking her to death, but refrained, just barely.

"And...?" I prompted her.

"She may have had a child when she was around twenty."

"What? Why, that's great!" I shouted leaping up out of my chair and almost hugging her.

"Like I said, we've not verified it yet. It's still just a rumor at this point."

"Tell me more," I demanded.

"Well, there's not a lot more to tell," she replied. "If she had the baby, it was out of wedlock and it was probably conceived during the summer she spent in Haight-Ashbury. Rumor has it that she came home with a 'bun in the oven' and refused to have an abortion or put the child up for adoption, and she would never divulge who the father might have been, even to her family."

"Oh, it gets richer by the moment." It took everything I had to not dance around the room, but my journalistic professionalism kept my feet in check. "Anything else?"

Deanna shook her head. "Not yet."

"Any idea where this mystery child might be? Is it a girl or boy? We really need to know who the father is as well. Can you find that out?"

"Whoa, hold your horses, Tonto," Deanna said. "Like I've said already, it's only rumor at this point. I've got Veronica and Diane on it."

"Who are they?" I asked.

"They're our two new interns. I swear, if you'd come down into the trenches every now and..."

"No, no, no," I interrupted her. "Not interns. I need the best on this story. Fiona still works for me, doesn't she? Put her on it."

"Are you sure? She's working on several other leads right now..."

"Yes, I'm sure," I interrupted again. "Take her off everything else, and put her on this and give her the two interns as well."

Deanna sighed heavily. "You're the boss," she said, then as she turned to leave, I'm pretty sure I heard, "at least for a few more days."

But I didn't care. Angeline Tarkington might have had a baby out of wedlock. Social media would eat this up.

I sat back down at my desk. *What if I let the rumor leak?* I thought. But I knew better than to go down that tunnel. If I did, I'd have Dottie to answer to every Friday night for the rest of my life. Or worse, she might never visit me again.

The Triumvirate

THE FAKE NEWS RUMORS that I'm some puppet to the power brokers of the world are RIDICULOUS. I'm no puppet. I'm one of the most (maybe the most) powerful men in the world. So relax. I'll take good care of you. Tweet by President Oscar Wellian

HONORABLE #1 POINTED the remote at the screen and switched it off. The lights in the plush viewing room immediately came on, leaving the three men blinking to adjust their eyes. A lone butler stood at the ready, discreetly out of the way, but close to the fully stocked bar in case any of the three most powerful men in the world needed their drinks refreshed. Behind the oldest of the three, who sat in a motorized wheelchair, stood a tall, slender nurse in her white uniform, who stifled a yawn as she glanced at her watch and frowned.

"Well, I can tell Margaret is glad to see the debate finally end," Honorable #1 quipped.

The nurse nodded, embarrassed to be noticed by the informal head of the Military Industrial Complex or M.I.C. for short. "I apologize. My son kept me awake last night with a bad cold."

"Hey, Honorable #3, when are you Big Pharma guys going to finally find a cure for the common cold?"

"Probably never," the old man in the wheelchair replied with a raspy voice that sounded like he had his own respiratory ailments. "Too much profit in treating the symptoms."

"Yeah, that's no doubt true," Honorable #1 agreed. He raised his glass and Banyon, the butler, was instantly at his side with a bottle of Château du Tariquet, refilling his glass. "Well, what are your assessments on this first of way too many debates?"

"Nothing particularly surprising, as far as I could tell," Honorable #2 replied. He was a tall, slender man whose dark skin contrasted with the white of his thawb. "Of course, it's early, but I'd say OPEC has nothing to worry about from any of these folks. Besides, most of them will scurry back into their respective holes in the next few weeks. And we have the frontrunners well in line, correct?"

"Of course we do. We have all our bases covered as far as that's concerned," Honorable #1 assured the other two men.

"Who was that last woman, and where in the world did that question Roberta asked come from? It certainly wasn't on the list I saw," Honorable #2 asked, as he also motioned to Banyon to fill his glass with water.

"That was Angeline Tarkington. A nobody, really," Honorable #1 said. "She just barely made it on the stage. Really, a non-issue."

"I'm not so sure," Honorable #3 said, as he took a handkerchief from his jacket pocket and wiped his nose. "I thought I recognized her name, so I Googled her when she made the cut for the debate. She's big in the alternative health field and has quite a following from her books and speaking tours. A nut job for sure, but we don't want to ignore anyone at this point. Remember what happened last election."

They all laughed. "Well, yes, but that took a tremendous amount of hard work and mega bucks to make that happen. That's not going to happen this go around and especially not with her," Honorable #2 said. "You're not suggesting we back..."

"No, don't be ridiculous," Honorable #3 replied. "I want one more drink before we wind this up tonight." He glanced at his nurse, who frowned sternly at him, but refrained from saying anything. When Banyon had finished topping off his drink, Honorable #1 raised his glass for a toast. "Here's to a smooth campaign, and may the best man win!" They raised their glasses and chuckled at the remark. Of course, the best man would win. That's how it had always been and would remain so as long as they were in control of the puppet strings.

ANGELINE STROLLED INTO the sunroom of her L. A. home after a hectic week of campaigning that included over a dozen appearances on both regional and national talk shows. She had gotten a good night's sleep and was now ready for another day, but not until she completed one task that she'd been avoiding for weeks, but knew she could avoid no longer.

She wore her favorite prayer shawl and had abstained from any alcohol or meat of any kind for the last forty-eight hours in preparation for this time. She'd made sure that her staff knew she was not to be disturbed until she had finished "checking in with the Source", as she described it. All her staff had been with her long enough to know what that meant, even if they didn't fully believe or understand it. They would in good time. All would in perfect time.

She strolled around the room for a few minutes, enjoying the feeling of being home after so many days on the road. She loved her home, having spent the last twelve years here whenever she wasn't on the road speaking. Some of her best books had been written here, and she would regret leaving it for that white monstrosity in D. C. *But let's not get ahead of ourselves,* she thought. First things first, step by step, and this next step today was an important one.

She walked over to the altar and sat down in front of it cross-legged. Even though she'd meditated in such a position almost every day for the past twenty years, she had noticed lately that it was getting a little more difficult. Lengthy meditations were becoming increasingly uncomfortable, but some habits are hard to break and well worth continuing despite becoming harder.

She leaned over and lit a candle as she began breathing slowly in through her nose for a count of six and then exhaling through her mouth for the same length of time. She let her eyelids relax but did not completely close her eyes. Despite being rested, she didn't want to run the risk of falling asleep. After a minute or two, she reached into the pocket of her robe and removed the three photos of the subject for today's process. She opened her eyes just a bit in order to take a final look at the image of a much younger Oscar Wellian taken while in grade school, a second picture of his graduation from college and a recent snapshot of him as President that one of her staff had downloaded from the internet. She placed them on the altar and closed her eyes again. As much as she had been dreading this moment, it was time to step into his world and to see reality through his eyes.

Breathe. Remember, keep breathing, she told herself, as she slipped out of her world and into Wellian's.

It would take her days to recover.

The Field Narrows

I FOUND THE PERFECT remedy for insomnia. Try watching the Democratic debate. Snoring within minutes. Tweet by President Oscar Wellian

A FEW WEEK'S AFTER the first debate, the DNC released the criteria and dates for the second debate, increasing the number of unique contributors needed as well as the dollar amount. Upon reading this in the *Washington Post*, I glanced over to Cynthia, who was waiting for me to finish so we could look at the schedule for the day.

"Too bad," I said, as I dropped the paper on my desk. "No doubt that will narrow the field considerably, including knocking Tarkington off the stage for next time."

"Maybe," Cynthia replied with a coy smile on her face.

"You know something I don't?" I asked. "Like the Russians are backing her, or someone else overseas?"

"Don't be ridiculous. Angeline Tarkington would never allow such a thing as that. She's a woman of high integrity."

"Really?" I considered the statement for a moment before continuing. "Okay, I'll grant you that for discussion purposes, but it's going to take a lot more than that to pull off a virtual nobody making the cut this go around. That's especially true when the little media coverage she's getting refers to her as a fringe candidate."

"Well, all I'm saying at this point is to not count her out quite yet. She may have some angels helping her out," Cynthia replied. "Now, can we get on with scheduling the day? I actually have work to do."

"Whoa, wait a minute. What's that last statement supposed to mean? Angels? Like from heaven, those kinds of angels?"

Cynthia raised one hand to her lips and made a motion as though locking them tight, and try as I might I couldn't get any more out of her.

Needless to say, it turns out she was right twice over. Angeline Tarkington did just make the cut and it was due to her angels. What I didn't know at the time was that she had a large and loyal following of men and women who'd been following her work for decades and who had recently dubbed themselves Angeline's Angels. They flooded social media with her message and enrolled many of their friends into contributing to her campaign. Angeline Tarkington would be one of the twelve candidates in the second debate being moderated by CNN.

Turns out that Cynthia, my all to perky assistant, was one of Angeline Tarkington's most enthusiastic Angels.

HONORABLE #2 WALKED into Honorable #1's office a few minutes prior to their scheduled quarterly meeting, with Honorable #3 right behind him.

"Take a look at these," Honorable #2 said, as he handed two tablets to Honorable #1.

"What are they?" Honorable #1 asked, as he took them and set them on his desk.

"Read them," Honorable #2 instructed.

Honorable #1 took a pair of reading glasses out of his pocket and put them on before picking up the two tablets. After glancing at one and then the other, he said, "They're the same, aren't they? No, wait." He looked closer. "They aren't the same." He paused and read the first couple paragraphs on one, then moved over to the other one and read the same paragraphs.

He looked up and over to Honorable #2. "Who wrote these?"

"Ernest," Honorable #2 replied.

Honorable #1 groaned. "My nephew-in-law, Ernest, the one on the Divisive Team?"

"The very same," Honorable #2 replied.

"But why?"

"You'll need to ask him," Honorable #3 inserted.

"Well, I will."

"Let us know what he says, and what we should do about it. That team is too important to our overall mission to be playing around with it."

Ernest Heathrow stepped into his uncle's office. "You asked to see me, Unc?"

"Yes, come in, boy. I have something I think you'll find of interest."

"What's that?"

Honorable #1 pointed to the two newspapers on his desk, both turned to the op-ed page. "Did you write these?"

Ernest glanced down at the two papers, then back up to his uncle with a smile on his face and nodded. "Yes, I did," he replied, with a note of pride in his voice.

"And why, might I ask, did you use the same pattern and format, but the exact opposite content?"

"To see if I could," Ernest replied without hesitation. "Also, I wanted to see what the results would be. I think the exercise turned out quite well. Don't you?"

"Exercise?"

"Sure," Ernest replied. "Writing just hyper-conservative opinion pieces was getting boring, so even though I knew we have other members on the Divisive Team that write hyper-progressive pieces, I thought it would be fun and instructional to see if I couldn't walk in both worlds and write from both perspectives." He pointed to the two newspapers. "That's the result. Why, what's the problem, Unc?

Honorable #1 glared at the young man, who'd been a thorn in his side for years, before answering. "What if someone else notices the similarities in style? The Divisive Team could be unmasked, and that would be disastrous. If the masses realized how we've been using the mainstream media for years to keep them at each other's throats..." He left the thought hanging.

"Yeah, I know, divide and conquer, right?"

"Exactly, but it only works as long as no one knows we're doing it by design."

Ernest thought about that for a moment. "True, but I wouldn't worry about it. No one is going to notice because we've already done such a good job of dividing and conquering. Someone who enjoys reading hyper-conservative opinion pieces isn't going to read hyper-progressive op-eds and vice versa. Really, don't worry, Unc. We're in the clear."

Brasten opened the stack of newspapers one by one, turning each to the Op-Ed section—his Sunday ritual in an effort to keep a pulse on the mood of Amberica's citizens. He read over one after another as he sipped on his coffee, occasionally dipping the crust of his dry toast in it. It all read pretty much the same as it had for years. A lot of anger mixed with fear...until...

"Wait a minute. Didn't I just read this one?" He looked through the stack of already read papers until he found the Op-Ed he was looking for. No, it couldn't be the same. The paper was one of the most conservative ones around, and this new piece was anything but conservative. So, why had it felt so familiar? He spread the two papers out next to each other so he could compare them. "I'll be darned. Are you kidding me?" He rubbed his chin considering. "What's going on here?" He picked up the phone to call the Op-Ed editors of both papers. *Something is rotten in the state of Denmark*, he thought, as he waited for someone to pick up on the other end.

Moral Compass

WITH OVER TWO DOZEN Democratic candidates now running against me, there's not one that has a chance. So sad. Tweet by President Oscar Wellian

IT HAD BEEN A PARTICULARLY grinding sort of week with Edward once more on his rant about declining ratings, so I decided to head out to the little farm in the western part of the state where Dottie and I had planned to retire one day. As I pulled in under the carport, I realized it'd been at least six months since I'd been there, which meant it'd probably been closer to a year, and yet it felt like coming home for some reason. I got out of the car, reached into the back seat for my suitcase and the bag of booze. I couldn't remember what supply I still had here and didn't want to take any chances.

I stood there next to the car with the bag in hand and the suitcase next to me, took a few deep breaths of the mountain air and listened to the crickets off in the distance as Rufus climbed out of the back seat and relieved himself on a nearby bush. So much for the hustle bustle sounds of the city. *I should come here more often,* I thought, then remembered that's exactly what I'd thought last time. *I guess I'll have to add this to my list of things that worked so well I quit doing them.*

As I suspected, the supplies were limited, both in the liquor cabinet and the freezer, but I did find a frozen steak and a bag of frostbitten fries that would keep me from starving until I could get into town in the morning.

I fixed myself an Old Fashioned as the steak and potatoes were defrosting in the microwave. By the time the food was ready and I walked out to the deck to eat it, I was on my third drink on an empty stomach and feeling no pain. Meanwhile, Rufus had already retired to the bedroom for the night. He tended to sleep even more in the cool mountain air.

It was around my fourth or fifth drink when I heard the four words that all husbands most dread: "We need to talk."

Oh, oh. What have I done now? I thought, as I glanced around to see Dottie sitting in the swing at the end of the deck. "Really? I didn't expect to see you tonight. I thought I'd given you the slip and left you in New York." I glanced into the living room at the bottle sitting on the counter. *It's your fault.* But I knew better. I was the one who fixed the drinks.

"Why are you trying to undermine Angeline Tarkington's campaign?" Dottie asked.

"What?" I replied. "What are you doing following politics? You never seemed to have an interest in the past."

"My country wasn't in the hands of a narcissistic, psychopathic, lying puppet." The words tumbled out of her mouth.

"Wow, but how do you really feel about the POTUS?"

"I'm worried and so should you be. And so I repeat my question: Why are you undermining the one person who could defeat him and bring our country back to true North?"

"Whoa, wait just a minute. Are we still talking about the same person? Angeline Tarkington? Really?"

Dottie continued swinging despite having no way I could see that she could be propelling herself. After another moment, she stopped swinging, again with no indication of how. "Must I remind you how impressed you were with her after that interview years ago?"

"I really don't recall. Besides, what does that have to do with today?"

"You couldn't stop talking about her. You even said way back then, 'She needs to run for President. If she did, I'd vote for her.' What happened to that guy?"

"He sobered up?" The comment was as much a question as a statement.

"No, you weren't drinking or doing drugs in those days. You were still very much alive and believed in something. Again, what happened to that guy?"

"He died!" I shouted, pushing back my chair, which fell over with a bang. I charged towards the swing, then stopped. "Or rather, his wife died, leaving him all alone."

Dottie continued sitting there with a slight smile on her face, unfazed by my dramatics. "I know, sweetie," she finally said. "That was very unfair of me, but God had other plans, and so She called me home. But I never left you. I'm here with you now, aren't I?"

I shrugged. "Yeah, I guess." I turned around, walked back over to the chair and picked it up. I dragged it over closer to the swing and straddled it with my arms resting on its back.

"Well, you may as well keep your options open, just in case you find that other version of you and he still wants to vote for her. For that to happen, you have to make sure she's on the ballot come November."

"But, I can't do that! I'm a journalist, a political pundit," I whined.

"Please don't give me that hogwash. The least you can do is quit sabotaging her." She stood up and walked over to my chair, and I swear I could smell the sweet fragrance of the perfume she always wore. It brought tears to my eyes. "And maybe, just maybe, you could call in a few of those 'favor chips' you've been collecting over the years." She blew me a kiss and started to fade away, but before she disappeared entirely she added, "Oh, and how about trying to be a little less of an ass when you interview her again?"

"I didn't know I was...wait a minute. What do you mean, not be an ass?"

"Just that. Pretending you don't know what I'm talking about just to see if you can get a rise out of me. Asshole." And with that, she disappeared into the night.

Weekend Getaway

THE ECONOMY IS BOOMING and especially the stock market. No need to thank me. It's what I do. I'm a natural at it. Tweet by President Oscar Wellian

I WOKE UP ON SATURDAY morning with a familiar splitting headache and the taste of rotten potatoes in my mouth, both of which took the edge off of my enjoying a gorgeous sunlit day. I stumbled to the bathroom, relieved myself, popped three aspirins in my mouth, took a large swig of mouthwash, then gargled for several seconds before swallowing it all. My theory was that swallowing the mouthwash would not only freshen my breath and eliminate the gross taste, but would also dissolve the aspirins so they could do their magic that much faster. I climbed into the shower and took an invigoratingly cold one before shuffling into the kitchen to put on a pot of coffee.

By the time I'd finished my second cup of black joe, I was pretty sure I was going to survive another day. I checked my phone and confirmed what I already knew. No bars. Absolutely no contact with the outside world for the next two days, a complete news fast, just what the doctor had ordered, or would have ordered if I believed in going to doctors, which for the most part I did not, despite having excellent health insurance provided by the network.

I put on a clean t-shirt, a pair of jeans and tennis shoes. I called to Rufus, who'd slept under the bed. He slowly crawled out, shook himself, then joined me on a walk around the grounds. *Now, this is the life,* I thought, as I strolled down to the lake to check on the boats, a small fishing skiff and an ancient canoe. Both seemed to have survived the winter okay inside the small boathouse. *Why didn't I just move here? After all, I'm a writer. I could retire here and write my memoirs. Go ahead and turn in my 401-K. Worst case scenario, if I couldn't sell the book, I could simply blow my brains out here in relative peace.*

The thought of suicide stopped me in my tracks. Had my life deteriorated so much that I was ready to end it all? *No, not unless the book doesn't sell.*

Don't be a smart ass, I countered, now really concerned about my own mental health. *Everyone has a passing thought from time to time about ending it all, don't they? It's when you start taking action that you need to be worried.*

Wait, just a minute! What had been the last thing I'd done before climbing in the car and fastening my seatbelt? I'd checked the glove compartment to make sure the .44 Magnum was still there and loaded! *Holy shit! Is that what this is? A final trip to paradise before ending it all?*

By this time, I had broken out in a cold sweat. This was a serious wake up call. I turned around, looking for Rufus. "Come here, boy." I heard the sound of his ID tag against his collar and saw him jogging towards me. As he approached me with his tail wagging and his tongue sticking out to one side, I bent down and hugged him and cried into the soft fur of his neck.

I'm not sure how long I stayed that way—long enough that when I finally released Rufus, I had a catch in my back that hurt like hell, and I had Rufus's hair stuck to my face by the dried tears. In short, I was a mess. Clearly, it was time for me to take an inventory of my life. I patted my back pocket and was relieved to find my writing pad and pen. Some old habits never die. I walked to the end of the deck and kicked off my shoes. I sat down and hung my legs over the edge into the cool water.

At the top of one page, I wrote out the word "Pros" and on a second page wrote out "Cons". *Let's start with all the things that are working in my life,* I thought as I turned back to the Pros page.

I have a good job that pays well.

Great start. I thought for another moment before writing down: I have very little debt. *That's a real plus when you consider how many people are upside down in debt.*

I sucked on the end of the pen as thought for another minute or two, finally adding: I have a late model car that I enjoy driving and that is almost paid for.

I'm on a roll now, I thought, as I read over the list. I placed the pen's ballpoint down underneath the last item, ready to add another plus, but then couldn't come up with anything. *Fair enough. I'll come back to this list in a moment. Let's look at the Cons.* I was about to flip over to that page when Rufus came bounding out of the bushes, lumbered down the deck and leapt into the water, spraying me from head to knees.

"Rufus, no! Bad dog!" I yelled at him, and then laughed. I straightened myself up and wrote: I have a crazy old dog that loves me and makes me laugh.

Now, I was ready to take an objective look at the darker side of my life.

What wasn't working about my life that would cause me, even for a brief moment, to have thoughts of ending it?

I hate my job, no matter how much it pays.

I spend way too many hours at work and much of that time I'm either stretching the truth (we call it spin in the trade) or downright lying.

I have almost no friends except those at work, and

I know very little about them outside of work, and

I don't really care to know about them.

Okay, breathe. I found it refreshing to have been honest at least with myself. I thought another moment before adding,

I'm alone except for Rufus and I'm often lonely and depressed, and

I drink way too much, and

I have difficulty sleeping, and

I'm at least 20, no 30 pounds overweight, and

At the end of the day I have very little energy.

Keep breathing.

I haven't had sex since...*When was the last time I'd slept with a woman?* I couldn't remember... a very long time, and I missed it. Not just the physical release that it provided, but the closeness and intimacy of it all. *Boy, was that the truth.* I felt a tear trickle down one cheek, followed a second later by another one on the other side.

I took three deep breaths and slowly let them out before writing: I have no purpose to my life. I'm not living, merely existing.

An image of the .44 Magnum lying in the glove compartment flashed in my mind, accompanied a second later by the thought, *Why wait for the book to flop? Let's just get it over with now.*

And in that moment, God intervened in the form of a lumbering, smelly, wet dog. Rufus climbed out of the water onto the deck beside me and shook himself, spraying me for the second time.

"Rufus!" I leaned away from the liquid assault and almost fell in. *Yeah, Rufus. Who will take care of him if I propel an ounce of lead through my brain?*

No, suicide wasn't the answer. It was way too easy, and when had I ever taken the easy path? But clearly the life inventory did not lie. I had hardly a half page of *Pros* and over two pages of *Cons.* Clearly, I needed help. Rufus came over to me and nuzzled my neck. I reached over to the water-soaked dog and hugged him, then used his sturdy body to help me stand up.

"Let's go grocery shopping, boy," I said, as I started walking back to the cabin. Since I wasn't going to take my own life, at least not this day, I might as well go get us both some good food to eat.

Get Her Back

HALF THE DEM (OR IS it dim) candidates have dropped out of the race, no doubt realizing they don't have a chance running against me. Tweet by President Oscar Wellian

YOU MIGHT HAVE THOUGHT that such an intimate reckoning with my own dark side would have led me to turn my life around. You know, go to the grocery store and buy only organic fruits and vegetables, and the best cuts of beef, but only for Rufus. Then go home and pour all the booze down the drain and drink only spring water. Well, that kind of turnaround happens only in books. Remember, I don't ever take the easy path. In my defense, I did buy the best cuts of beef and shared them with Rufus, but the rest of the grocery run was junk food city—all highly processed, pre-packaged comfort food. You know, my normal diet. And I did pour the booze...down my throat. In fact, I stayed drunk most of the rest of the weekend until mid-afternoon on Sunday, when I knew I had to stop so I could drive back to the city. The funny thing was that, despite being drunk, I didn't see Dottie the rest of the weekend. Had even she given up on me? Was it going to be just Rufus and me for the rest of my life? I have to confess, I missed the ol' girl, even if she was a ghost or a figment of my demented imagination.

But something did change come Monday morning. I had a mission. Maybe not quite a whole new purpose in life, but a mission—a directive straight from the spirit world. Dottie had been right. I'd been unnecessarily brutal and unfair with Angeline Tarkington, as had the rest of the mainstream media community. I could turn that around, or at least I could give it the good old college try. *Maybe if I'm successful, Dottie will return,* I thought as I walked into Edward's office. Then I chided myself, *Really, I'm going to bust my balls and put my career on the line in the hopes my ghost of a wife will return and make me feel guilty about how hopeless my life has become since her passing? Is that the level to which I've sunk? Yes, it is!*

I didn't bother to knock on Edward's door but strolled in unannounced. I often found this a good strategy when I wanted to get my way. It keeps people off balance. It certainly worked in Edward's case.

"Man, you look like shit," Edward said, as he dropped his pen on the paperwork on his desk and leaned back in his chair.

"Thanks for the compliment," I replied. I stepped right up to the edge of the desk and leaned over at him. "I want her back on the show." I looked him straight in the eyes as I said it and refused to blink.

"Whoa, your breath would sink a ship," Edward replied. He reached into his desk drawer and pulled out a package of mints. "Here, suck on a couple of these and feel free to keep the pack. It's the least I can do for my co-workers."

I took the pack and popped two of the lozenges in my mouth, then turned back to him. "Well, will you book her this week?"

He stared at me with a look of incredulity on his face. "Are you kidding me? You're not talking about Angeline Tarkington, are you? You are, aren't you? What's with this dame and you? You're not having an affair with her, are you?"

"Don't be ridiculous," I replied. "Though, technically, it wouldn't be called an affair since I'm no longer married and she's unmarried. It would be called 'dating'."

"It would be called career and political suicide. It would be called sleeping with the enemy. It would be called..."

"Okay, okay, I get your point, but no, I'm not doing anything like that. I just find her an engaging and thoughtful guest, and each time she's on our show, we get a nice spike in the ratings." I didn't have a clue whether that was true or not but thought it worth taking a shot. "It's the show that I'm focused on, and you and I making it the best it can be."

Edward cocked his head to one side with a look that reminded me of Rufus when he thinks he hears something outside. He studied me for several seconds like I was some alien from another planet that had just stepped into his office. Finally, he said, "What's really going on here, Brasten? You've been weirder than usual. Are you okay? Do you need to take some time off? That can be arranged. Lord knows you've covered for enough people through the years. You could redeem some of those favors you've collected."

Strange, that's exactly what Dottie had suggested I do, but for another purpose.
"No, no, I'm fine," I replied.

"Well, in that case how about we book some of the other eleven candidates that are still in the race. You know, the men and women who all have a lot more political experience and who have a chance to make this next election a real race."

"No, look, if you book Tarkington on the show, I promise we'll see a huge spike in the ratings..."

"Don't go there again," Edward said, interrupting me. "That dog won't hunt a second time. I'd really have to fire you next time."

"Um, well," I replied. *Come on, Brasten, think of something fast, or you're going to lose him.* "You want the truth? Here's the thing. I want Angeline Tarkington back on the show because no one else has given her the opportunity to share her unique views and perspective, and I think the Amberican public have the right to hear what she has to say. I'm not saying she should be our next President. That's not our decision to make. That's for the public to decide come election day. I do think it is our job to be sure everyone who's running for the highest office in the land has a fair shake to be heard." I paused to catch my breath and realized I had actually said the truth, at least my own truth, for the first time in a long time. I smiled at my producer and waited for his reply.

"You really are so full of shit that I don't quite know what to make of it," Edward finally said. "I don't believe you believe a word of what you just said, but...," he held up one finger to keep me from interrupting him, "...I believe that is an integral part of our job, one that we often fall down on, so in this case, I'll give you what you want. I'll have Cynthia give her campaign manager a call today."

I let out a breath I hadn't realized I'd been holding. I started around the desk to either shake Edward's hand or give him a hug. I wasn't sure which, but before I made it around, he stopped me. "The mints aren't working. How about going out and buying yourself a toothbrush and toothpaste, maybe some mouthwash as well. Now, get out of here. I have work to do."

I nodded and left. I sent Cynthia out to the pharmacy for the supplies.

"SHE WHAT?! ARE YOU kidding me?" I blurted, staring at Cynthia with a shocked look on my face.

"Nope," Cynthia replied. "She said she appreciated the invitation but respectfully declines. Actually, that's what Stella, her campaign manager, said."

"Well, I'm sorry. I don't accept her decline. Get Stella on the phone," I ordered.

Cynthia nodded and ran from the office, happy to escape from my wrath.

A few minutes later, she used the intercom, which she almost never did, to let me know that Stella was on the line.

"Thanks for taking my call," I said, then launched right into my spiel. "Stella, you've got to change her mind and have her appear on my show. You know CNN won't give her any air time to speak of. At least on my show, she'll get the opportunity to share her ideas and beliefs."

"Like whether or not she believes in ghosts?" Stella asked, with an icy edge to her voice.

"Okay, fair enough, but I promise not to ask her such questions. In fact, you tell me what questions to ask. I'll give you three, no, four questions, and I promise to ask them during the interview."

There was a long silence on the other end. "Really? You'd do that?"

"Promise," I replied. "Now, I will press her on them and anything else that comes up. Fair?"

After another pause, I heard a deep sigh. "I'll talk to her and let you know before the end of the day."

"Great! Thanks." I hung up the phone, then picked it back up to make another call. "What's the latest you have on Angeline Tarkington's mystery child? Well, I want everything you have on my desk by the end of the day."

Interview #3

DO WE HAVE A MYSTIC running for my position? Flipping through to Fox I caught a snippet of MSNBC. 'The spirit of the divine?' Really? Tweet by President Oscar Wellian

IT HAD BEEN A GOOD show thus far with no gaffs or unexpected surprises, and I could see the finish line with just one more question to ask candidate Tarkington when we came back from the break. Our makeup lady had taken Angeline off stage to powder her nose or something like that, so I sat there alone, praying she'd be back on stage before the camera light flashed red. She made it with fifteen seconds to spare.

The light flashed and I went into talk-show mode. "Welcome back for our last segment, and thank you, Ms. Tarkington, for staying."

"Happy to do so," she said, smiling warmly, which she'd done throuhout the show, even when I'd pressed her pretty hard on a few of the followup questions. No question about it, she was one cool cucumber, or as I'm sure Dottie would describe her, 'a centered human being'. In either case, I was interested to see how she responded to my last question.

"As we close for the evening, I have just one more question for you. For whose benefit are you running for the presidency of Amberica? Would you speak directly to them tonight?"

Angeline turned to face the camera, her warm smile growing a bit more serious. "There are people in this country who are hurting. I'm not just talking about our poor, or our minorities, many of whom haven't received a fair chance in decades. No, there are many others who, from all outward appearance, are doing fine. They're financially stable, with a good job, even though it's corrupting their spirit. If you asked this 'silent majority', they'd be the first to tell you,

'Oh, yes, everything is fine.' But they are morally and spiritually bankrupt, and they are suffering mightily.

"You know the leading cause of death in this country? It's not heart disease, or cancer. It's suicide."

What? Wait a minute, that's not true, I thought. I was about to point out the inaccuracy, but before I could, Angeline went on.

"These cases of suicide often go undiagnosed. No, I mean suicide by auto accidents, by excessive drinking, through 'accidental' overdoses. These cases fly under the radar and yet are very real. It's time for us to start speaking the truth—not just speaking truth to power, but also the truth of the most power-ful...the spirit of the Divine within us all. If we don't, many of our citizens will take their own lives in ways that won't be reported as suicides, but their families and loved ones will know, and they will experience the loss just as deeply.

"And those are the people for whom I'm running to be President."

I sat there for several seconds, even while Edward screamed in my ear to sign off. *She's talking about me,* I thought, as I stared at her with a whole new appreciation. Then, the next realization caught my breath. *I'm one of the people that has her in this race.*

I finally caught Edward from the wings jumping up and down to get my at-tention and giving me the signal to end the show by sweeping one hand across his throat.

I started to sign off with my regular tagline, "Are you kidding me...?", but then stopped. For some reason, it seemed completely inappropriate. Instead, I reached out my hand to my guest. "Thank you for being on the show tonight." As our hands touched, I felt a wave of loving energy course up my arm and straight to my heart.

Angeline smiled and nodded. "Thanks for having me," she said, then added, as nonchalantly as you please, "Please say hi to Dottie next time you see her."

I sat there stunned by the comment. How was it possible she knew that I referred to my wife as Dottie? That had been our little secret—we'd never told anyone. I had tried using it once shortly after we were married, but she'd have nothing to do with it. "You can call me that when I'm dead and gone, but not before," she'd warned me. It had become a game for us and an endearing word after her death.

"Cut, that's a wrap," I heard Edward say as he strolled on stage, though it sounded muffled and distant, like he was in the next room. I continued to hold Angeline's soft hand as we gazed into each other's eyes, not in a sexual or even loving way, but more like we were actually seeing each other for the first time.

"That was a great last segment," Edward continued, oblivious that the two people to whom he was speaking were in the midst of having a moment. Finally, Angeline squeezed my hand and patted it with her other one before letting go and turning her attention to my producer.

The two of them stood there for a few minutes talking while I continued to sit mesmerized by the realization I'd just had. I tried to remember the last time I felt like a presidential candidate was actually running for me, that they even cared about people like me. The only one that came to mind during my lifetime was Kennedy, and look what they'd done to him. I quickly glanced over to Angeline. *You are in grave danger,* I thought. Then, *Stop that silly thinking. She's not actually going to make it far enough to be in danger.* But there was some part of me deep inside that wasn't convinced.

Just then, Cynthia stormed onto the set with all her overly zealous energy, waving a sheet of paper.

"The prelim numbers are in," she said, as she stopped next to Edward. "Want to see them?"

Of course he does, dodo. He lives for those prelim numbers. They were early indications of how well all the shows had gone that evening.

He took the paper from her and glanced at them, then took a closer look. "Wait a minute. Is this a joke? These can't be right." He pointed to the bottom of the page.

"That's what I thought too," Cynthia replied, "So I had them checked again."

"We had a double-digit increase in tonight's show? Really?"

Cynthia nodded, smiling from ear to ear. "Really!" As she walked past me, I heard her whisper, "Don't underestimate the power of Angels to make a difference."

HONORABLE #1 FLIPPED off the TV that covered one full wall of the viewing room and turned to Banyon.

"Get the other two on the line."

"I took the liberty of doing so," Banyon replied. "They're waiting for you. Shall I place them on the screen?"

"Yes, please."

A moment later, the two men appeared, each taking up half the screen, with a smaller image of Honorable #1 in the lower right hand corner.

"Did you see the show tonight?" Honorable #1 asked, getting right to the point.

"Yes," the two men replied.

"Well, what did you think?"

Honorable #2 spoke first. "Not much to say, really. The woman is articulate, but so are the other candidates. Well, Senator O'Hare could use a few speech lessons, but we knew that going in."

"I agree," Honorable #3 replied. "I don't see any real threat here. She's a flash in the pan. She's getting almost no coverage on the other stations, so what's the big deal?"

Honorable #1 motioned to Banyon for a drink. "I'm not so sure. We've too much at stake not to cover all our bases." He steepled his fingers in front of his lips and closed his eyes. The other two waited, recognizing the sign that he was deep in thought. A moment later, he opened his eyes and glanced over to Banyon, who handed him the drink.

"I think it would be wise for us to do a little digging of our own, just to be absolutely sure."

The other two men nodded their agreement. "Never hurts to have a little dirt, just in case we need to sling it," Honorable #2 said.

"How about we put Sawyer and his team on it?" Honorable #3 added. "He's thorough and discrete."

Honorable #1 nodded, then took a long sip from his drink. He hoped it would help him sleep better tonight. "Okay, are we aligned?"

"Aligned," the other two replied in unison.

Honorable #1 flipped off the screen, finished his drink and went to bed, but not before calling their top private investigator.

Three days later Honorable #1 received word from Sawyer. "The subject in question may have had a child out of wedlock. It's not yet confirmed. I'm continuing to dig."

"Excellent," Honorable #1 replied. "Stay on it. I want daily briefs on what you find."

"You've got it," Sawyer replied.

Debate #2

NO NEED FOR FORGIVENESS here, Woo-woo Woman. My record is impeccable and right on in making Amberica great again. Tweet by President Oscar Wellian

ONCE AGAIN, SOCIAL media was filled with clips from Angeline Tarkington's appearance on *The Brass Brasten Show* with an even mixture of pros and cons on how she did. As I moved through my Twitter feed and then my Facebook posts, I began to see a pattern—one of Angeline's Angels would post something positive, with supporters liking or even loving it, then others would talk about how she didn't have a chance to become the Democrats' nominee, much less win against Wellian. Undoubtedly, the segment most often mentioned or shared was the final one in which the candidate identified for whom she was running.

So, I'm not the only one that resonated with, I thought, as I clicked off my phone. *Time to get back to work.* But before I could do so, Cynthia fluttered into my office like a sparrow who'd magically managed to slip into the building and couldn't find its way out.

"A little less flitting, if you please."

"Oh, and here I thought you'd be in better spirits after being in the presence of not just an Angel, but *the* Angel," Cynthia said.

"She's charismatic," I replied. "I'll give you that." *But an angel? I'm not so sure,* I thought, recalling the rumor of her having a baby and keeping it secret.

"Oh, for sure she's that and so much more," Cynthia continued, as she dropped a folder on my desk.

I picked it up and glanced at the label, then looked back at her with a quizzical look on my face. "What do I need this for?"

"Oh, you don't," Cynthia replied. "I just used it as an excuse to come see you."

"And when did you ever not barge in here with or without a reason?" I asked, handing her back the folder.

"Good point. Well, last night's show changes everything, doesn't it?"

"Why do you say that?"

"Surely CNN will have to give her more air time during the debate, won't they? If they don't, they'll look foolish."

I considered her point for a moment before replying. "Maybe, but CNN has never seemed to mind looking foolish before."

Cynthia pursed her lips. "True, but still, I say she'll get more attention. Just you wait and see."

Turns out, for once, I was right and Cynthia was wrong. CNN's debate moderators virtually ignored the Angel on stage, and I found myself disappointed to be right, which is very unlike me. Still, in the few opportunities she had to speak, she made the most of them, including her response to one question directed specifically at her.

"You've said several times in your speeches that a key step to bringing ourselves back to a moral center is forgiveness. If that's true, does that mean you'll forgive Wellian for the many actions and policies that you and others have identified as amoral?"

Angeline response was quick and to the point. "Yes, I pray for President Wellian every day and..."

"Excuse me? You pray for our President?" the moderator asked.

"Yes, of course, and I ask others to pray for him as well," Angeline replied. "And part of that prayer it to forgive him."

"Thank you..."

Angeline held up a finger and spoke on. "But let me make one thing perfectly clear about forgiveness. While it is an important and powerful spiritual and moral practice, to forgive someone does not mean we condone their actions. I do and will continue to forgive President Wellian for his actions, and when I'm the next President, I will hold him to account for those actions. Thank you for the question."

"What did she just say?" I asked Rufus, but he was sound asleep and snoring quietly. I backed up the segment and watched it again, then opened my laptop to find that an online firestorm had already begun, and it was less than ten minutes since the second debate had ended. The debate had lasted two hours, with the other eleven candidates taking up ninety-five percent of the time, but all of that had apparently been forgotten.

Five minutes later, my cellphone rang. I glanced at it long enough to see the call was from my producer, so I took it.

"You watched the debate, right?" *What a dumb question,* I thought, but decided not to aggravate him further. I could tell from the tone of his voice he was already peeved by something.

"Sure thing," I replied evenly, in an attempt to stay neutral until I figured out where Edward was heading.

"We've got to get her back on the show," Edward said. "I want you to ask her some straight questions to get this all sorted out."

"Like what?"

"Like how in the world can a candidate who's currently polling at less than two percent say something like 'When I'm the next President, I'll hold our current President to account for all his atrocities and misdeeds?"

I started to point out that wasn't exactly what she'd said, but then thought better of it. I knew that when Edward went off on such rants, the best thing to do was to pretend to listen until he burned himself out, so instead I said, "Yes, that would be an interesting question to ask. Do you think the big wigs upstairs will approve having her on the show again so soon?"

"I'll see that they do," Edward replied. "How about coming in on time tomorrow morning for a change? I want to go over the schedule and see who we can move to the following week."

"Will do," I replied and hung up.

The next morning I shuffled into my office at 8:45 to find sitting on my desk the mug of strong coffee that I'd called to request while driving in.

"Will you let Edward know that I'm in and available?" I asked Cynthia, as I passed by her desk.

She glanced at her watch, or where her watch would have been on her wrist if she wore one. "Wow! I didn't think anyone was allowed to let you out of your cage before ten."

I turned and growled at her menacingly, then proceeded to the lifeline of coffee. A few minutes later, Edward sauntered in and dropped into the chair across from my desk. I could tell from his body language that he wasn't happy about something.

"Trouble sleeping?" I hazarded a guess.

"No. Well, yeah, that too, but mainly I couldn't get the big wig to approve having Angeline Tarkington back on the show—your show or anyone else's."

"Really? What was his rationale?"

"He didn't say, not really. Kinda beat around the bush. We've had her on more than any other network. It's their turn, maybe later, but probably not. I couldn't get a straight answer."

I was surprised by my own level of disappointment over the news. I had already started thinking of other questions to ask, though the question I really wanted to ask would never make it on the show. "How do you know that my secret nickname for my dead wife is Dottie?"

Tell him about the mystery baby, a devilish side of me insisted. *That'll change the big wig's mind for sure.* And I realized it probably would, but then remembered the many lectures Edward had had with the staff over the years.

"Don't come to me with rumors of what might be going on in the world. That's why we have a huge team of topnotch researchers. Find out the facts, then bring those to me. No facts, no news."

So far, all I had were rumors and innuendo, and until I had some facts to back them up, it would be both unprofessional to bring the subject up to Edward and totally unfair to Tarkington. *And since when did you start giving a hoot about her?* the small, vicious voice asked.

I'm not sure, but I thought I heard a cheer from Dottie sitting in the spiritual bleachers, but it was too soft to be certain. In any case, I kept my mouth shut. Unfortunately, as it turned out, I wasn't the only one working on that story angle. Fox News never let a lack of facts keep them from airing a good story, whether it was true or not.

Wellian's Rally

HEADING DOWN SOUTH to be with my people, the fine working class of South Carolina, then on to Florida for some much needed rest. Being your PO-TUS is a tiring job. Tweet by President Oscar Wellian

PRESIDENT OSCAR WELLIAN looked out over the crowd of southern sympathizers and puffed out his chest a little more. *They love me,* he thought, *no doubt about it, and I love the uneducated people of South Carolina.*

He clasped his two hands over his head like a boxer who'd just knocked out his opponent, and the crowd cheered even louder, then started chanting: "Four more years, four more years, four more years."

Oh, you have no idea what I have planned. Four more years is just a drop in the bucket.

He allowed the chant to continue for several minutes before raising his hand again for silence, and then found himself disappointed when they quieted down so quickly.

"Just one more thing before I have to climb back on Air Force One and head down to Florida." He waited until the crowd was quiet enough to hear his last statements.

"Did any of you see the sitcom last night that they're calling the second Democratic debate?" A loud, low boo resonated through the hall. "No, no, really it was quite a show...if you're into slapstick, that is." The crowd laughed and cheered. After about thirty seconds, he raised his hands again for silence. "And what about that last question from Geraldine? What a piece of work she is, as is the entire team of CNN, the best fake news not worth wiping your...anyway...."

"And who the hell is this Angeline...Tarkingbush, is it? Talking Head?"

The crowd chuckled, and one lady behind him yelled, "It's Tarkington."

The rest of the crowd booed. "No, I'll tell you what her name is from now on. She's Woo-woo Woman, that's who she is."

Once again the crowd cheered, then started chanting, "Woo-woo Woman, Woo-woo Woman..." until Wellian raised his hand for silence. "I sure hope that's who the Dingbat Dems put up against me, but that'll never happen. Even the Dems aren't that crazy."

New York Times Editorial

DARK TIMES ABOUT TO hit for woesome Woo-woo woman. Tweet by President Oscar Wellian

I SAT IN THE BREAKFAST nook of my New York apartment, sipping on a second mug of coffee and munching on my dry toast, with a stack of the morning newspapers to my left. My morning-during-the-week routine rarely changed—even the pile of newspapers. Even though I had ready access to all of them on my smartphone, I still liked the feel of newsprint between my fingers. Plus, they made good liners for bird cages, not that I had any birds in cages. I'm too much of an animal lover to cage up a bunch of birds.

I turned to the Op-Ed section of the *New York Times*, where I found the surprising headline:

Why President Wellian Fears Angeline Tarkington

Really? Are you kidding me? It had become my morning mantra as much as my nightly send off. I read on:

President Oscar Wellian closed his poorly attended rally in Greenville, South Carolina last night by berating Democratic candidate Angeline Tarkington, but in the process, he may have revealed a dark secret that he's unlikely to admit to the media. Angeline Tarkington scares the bejesus out of him.

How do I know? Well, just look at who he always ends up giving derogatory nicknames to—the opposition that he most fears. So, while his Orwellian fans may have picked up the name Woo-woo Woman, and chanted it back to him, they may have missed just how afraid he is of the amount of damage a truly good person with deep spiritual roots could cause to the Evangelical portion of his base. Your day of reckoning may be closer than you think, Mr. President. By the way, have you ever noticed how close his name is to the term, Orwellian? O. Wellian? For those not familiar with the word, I'll save you the bother of

Googling it. It means: "characteristic of the writings of George Orwell, especially with reference to his dystopian account of a future totalitarian state in *Nineteen Eighty-Four.*"

How in the world did this slip through the New York Times editorial board? I wondered. I thought about calling Arthur Blain, my old boss and the current editor of the Op-Ed section, but then changed my mind. After all, it's still a free country, more or less, isn't it?

AS IS CUSTOMARY, I spent the first twenty minutes at work in the men's room, coffee and toast having finally kick-started my digestive tract back into action. It was also a good opportunity to check into social media, where I found that Angeline Tarkington continued to trend on Facebook and Twitter. According to several posts, people continued to Google her more than any other candidate despite the fact that the CNN moderators all but ignored her during the debate.

Could it be that this little woman was gaining some traction in her bid to become our next President of Amberica? Could she be building a bit of slow mo, as in momentum? *And what influence might her being on my talkshow three times have played?* Funny, I couldn't tell if that had come from my devilish self or maybe even from Dottie. I needn't have worried, for the positive mood I felt from what I'd learned that morning didn't last.

In fact, it was local Angel, Cynthia, that ruined it all when I stepped into my office with her close behind me.

"Do you wait in the shadows so you can ambush me?" I asked, as I sat down at my desk and looked for the mug of coffee that was supposed to be waiting for me but wasn't this morning.

"Ahh, no," Cynthia replied. "My desk is just outside. You walk by it every morning."

True enough, I thought. "What do you have there?" I asked, noticing she had a newspaper opened to one of the inside pages.

"I know the *New York Post* never makes it to your morning stack..."

"Ahh, no," I said, mocking her response to me. "That's because it's a terrible gossip rag, and I still have a thread of decency and integrity left in me."

"Really? Where?" Cynthia said, as she dropped the paper on my desk in front of me.

Angeline Tarkington NO Angel
Inside, The Love Child She's Never Claimed

Are you kidding me? I thought, as I glanced at the paper and up to Cynthia.

"Did you leak it to them?" I'd never heard so much malice and barely controlled anger from her.

"No, are you crazy? Why would I do that?"

"Bridgette is a friend of mine. You know Bridgette, right?"

I shook my head, a confused look on my face. "Refresh my memory."

"You're hopeless," Cynthia said, with just a hint less anger. "She's been on your research team for the last four years. We often go to lunch together. She told me what you've had them working on. She called it your pet project."

I groaned and reached for my coffee mug before realizing it wasn't in its customary spot. *I have to face all this without even coffee to bolster my courage? So unfair.* "Okay, hold your horses." I pointed to the paper. "This is one of the foremost trashy papers ever allowed to be published. I'm willing to bet you there are almost no facts in their story, but just rumor and speculation." *Wow, I'm now channeling Edward. This day is going from bad to horribly bad.*

"That's true," Cynthia replied. "I've read it and I circled all the statements that are factual." I opened the paper where she'd dog-eared the story and looked for the marks, but found only three: one stating the subject's name, a second stating that she'd grown up in Los Angeles, and the third that she'd spent a summer in Haight Ashbury.

"See, they have nothing to go on."

"But they don't have to," Cynthia said, almost crying now. "Do you know the circulation of this 'gossip rag?' It's over two hundred thousand, and that's not including the number of visits to their website every day. This is the worst kind of fake news, and it will be devastating to her and her campaign. And just when we were getting a little momentum going." She turned on her heels and stormed out of the office, leaving the paper behind.

So, I picked it up and read the whole thing, and felt my blood begin to boil. *This is the darker side of free speech,* I thought. Cynthia was right. The Conservative Right would have a field day with such a story.

Brasten Bottoms Out

A LOVE CHILD OUT OF wedlock by Woo-woo Woman? So reports the top news journal the New York Post. Who needs forgiveness now? Tweet by President Oscar Wellian

THE ARTICLE APPEARED in the *Post* on Wednesday morning and by Friday, several of the other candidates were calling for Angeline to withdraw her name as a Democratic candidate, and social media was on fire with posts and tweets both in favor of and against her continuing to remain in the race.

"She has to respond to these allegations in some way," I muttered to myself as I read some of the latest comments.

"Why do you say that?" Cynthia asked from my office doorway, where she'd just entered with the latest schedule changes in her hands.

"Because this isn't going away," I replied. "It's like a deep puncture wound. If it goes untreated, the infection will simply fester under the surface and eventually break out as a massive abscess."

"Oh, such a pretty picture you paint." She dropped the folder on my desk. "But won't that just keep the story alive for longer in the news cycle, especially since there's not a shred of evidence that any of it is true?"

I shook my head. "Not in this case." *Should I tell her that there actually is some evidence that my research team has begun to uncover? No, I swore Bridgette and the rest of the team to secrecy. Why would I break the silence now?* "This kind of dirt just feeds the Conservative Right and Wellian's base. They'll see to it that the story stays alive."

Cynthia nodded, but didn't say anything, then turned on her heel and walked out with a deep frown on her face. I opened the folder and glanced at the schedule changes for next week, then initialed them. I could only imagine how this change in events must be affecting my assistant. After all, she was one of Angeline's most loyal Angels. What I found surprising was how the news had affected *me*. Where had my journalistic neutrality disappeared to?

I glanced at the clock on the wall, which read 3 PM. I picked up the phone. It was time to cash in a favor or two and find someone who could cover my show tonight. I needed to get the hell out of Dodge.

By four o'clock, I'd found a replacement, then called and left a message to let Edward know I'd suddenly taken ill and would either see him on Monday or be in touch. I felt a real banger coming on.

As I drove west towards my cabin escape, I thought about the conversation I'd had with Olivia, the head of my research team. "We're pretty sure the story, at least some of it, is true."

"Pretty sure? You're the head of my research team. You need to know unequivocally, not just pretty sure. Get me what facts you have on my desk by Monday morning."

I stopped at my favorite liquor store on the way out of town and then broke one of my cardinal rules to never drink and drive. I twisted off the top of the Jack Daniel's and took a long draught. I wasn't waiting until I arrived at the cabin to start my weekend. My plan was to be well snockered by the time I pulled into the driveway. I reached and exceeded my goal, and if there are such things as angels, they were definitely looking after me and everyone else on the highway that evening. I barely reached the living room sofa before passing out.

I awoke the next morning shortly before noon with a fierce urge to pee. I stumbled into the bathroom to relieve myself and stumbled over Rufus, falling flat on my face, where I lay there dazed. I finally sat up and studied him where he'd retreated to the couch and was licking one paw. *How did he get himself inside?* I wondered. *For that matter, how did I get myself in?* Everything about the night before was hidden in a thick, drunken fog. I slowly stood up and rubbed my left knee that had taken the bulk of the fall. *Fine start to a new day*, I thought, as I continued my journey to the loo.

Afterwards, I fixed my regular breakfast of black coffee and dry toast. Knowing that my plan for the day and for the foreseeable future was to drink myself into oblivion, I decided to at least start out with a little something in my stomach. I made it to almost 1 PM before I took my first drink of the day. By mid-afternoon, I'd finished off my first bottle and cracked the seal on a second one. I don't remember much else about that day. Only that I was surprised and disappointed that Dottie hadn't bothered to pay me a visit somewhere along the way. The next twenty-four hours were a blur of drinking, then napping, drinking, passing out, drinking, throwing up, sleeping and drinking again.

It was somewhere in the midst of all this that Dottie came to see me, or perhaps it was me who made the journey to her this time, since I found myself sitting across from her, but not on a chair or stool. No, nothing so conventional. Instead, I sat on a cloud. No kidding, and as if that weren't bizarre enough, it was a pink cloud that looked and smelled exactly like the cotton candy I used to love eating at the State Fair each year as a child.

"So, are you planning to join me sooner rather than later?" Dottie asked, as I was still looking around, trying to get my bearings.

"What? Huh?" I returned my attention to her. "It looks like I already have."

"Don't be silly. This is just a dream...a dream of what is likely to come if you continue on your current path of self-destruction. You don't really think heaven is made up of clouds of cotton candy, do you?"

I shrugged. "It looks like at least some part of me does." I waved one hand to take in our surroundings.

"Well, that might be your idea of the afterlife. It's certainly not mine, but you're avoiding the question. Are you planning to come to me soon, like in the next few days or weeks?"

I shrugged again. "I don't know," I replied. "I haven't really thought about it. Maybe."

"Well, I strongly recommend you start thinking about it." Her voice took on an urgency I'd seldom heard from her. "And consider this. Where you're heading may not have the same zip code, big boy."

Her words sent a chill through me. I gulped at the thought, then asked, "You mean, all that drivel about there being a heaven and a hell is true?"

It was her turn to shrug. "I'm not at liberty to elaborate on that to you right now, given that you're still alive, though just barely. I had to ask special permission to even come to you in this way."

Special permission? From whom? I wondered, but before I could ask, she reached out with both of her hands and grasped mine.

"Please wake up. Wake up to what you are doing to yourself. You are in the process of committing the slow version of suicide. You know, the kind that rarely gets reported as someone taking their own life." She cocked her head and looked past me. "I've got to go. Please, take care of yourself, Brasten, my dear. Your work on Earth isn't complete yet. You have a significant difference to make before we're due to be reunited."

"Well, that's an interesting theory," I replied. "Care to elaborate on what that might be?"

But even as she shook her head, I could tell that our time was coming to an end as she started fading away. "Just wake up and pay attention. You'll figure it out."

I felt the warmth of her hands on mine slowly fade away, just as the rest of her did. I felt like my heart would break in that moment. Our love for each other was so palpable. And then I awoke.

Wake Up Call

AS WE APPROACH ELECTION Day, the Republican Party is more united than ever before. I look forward to being your President for another four years. Tweet by President Oscar Wellian

WHEN I AWOKE MIDDAY on Sunday, I had only a pint of cheap bourbon that I couldn't remember ever buying hiding in the deep corner of the liquor cabinet. Bad miscalculation. I'd drunk everything else and was now left with only the pint on the one day of the week that all the liquor stores were closed. Bummer.

Could this be a sign? I wondered, recalling the dream. I slowly made my way into the bathroom, whizzed and then turned on the shower, where I stayed until the hot water finally ran out. I've never been one to think much about my dreams. Most of them evaporate so fast anyway, and dream analysis was way too woo-woo for me. Only thing is that, as I toweled off, this particular dream was just as vivid as though it had actually happened. On top of that, I was surprised to find I felt almost human again, despite being faced with the dilemma of wanting to stay drunk but having nothing much to drink. *Yeah, that, and a clear, undeniable message from the hereafter,* I thought. In light of the dream, having next to no booze started seeming like more of a blessing than a curse. Almost.

As I sat at the kitchen table sipping on my black coffee, laced with just a little of the rot gut, I contemplated how to make it through the day, when a strange idea popped into my head—two, actually. The first was that I needed to somehow get back to my journalistic roots. Maybe that's where I'd finally fulfill my life purpose and could then join Dottie on the right side of the tracks. The second idea was even stranger. I wanted to take a bike ride around my little community, something I'd never been inclined to do in all the years I'd visited the area.

I'd bought a top class touring bike years ago, with a plan to become the fittest fifty-year-old on record, a goal that lasted about thirty minutes when I discovered how hard biking in the mountains really is. So, why did today seem like a good day to get it out of storage and tool around? I hadn't the foggiest. Even stranger, I had these two bizarre ideas tied together. I decided to take my pen and notebook, and the remaining pint of liquor, and go find me a story, just like the old days. Truth be known, I had never gone looking for a story on a bike, but, hey, my mind was playing weird tricks on me. I mean, heaven made of pink cotton candy?

I walked into the living room on my way to the storage shed and glanced at Rufus lying asleep on the couch. *Maybe I should take him with me,* I thought, but then the last shred of logic intervened. *Don't be silly. What are you going to do, put him in the bike basket, which, by the way, the bike doesn't have?* I left him asleep.

I was shocked to find the bike still in fairly good shape. It badly needed a good cleaning, the tires needed some air and the gears a good spraying of WD-40. In short order, presto, it was passable. I rolled it outside, jumped on and started weaving my way down the driveway. I figure I made it a good thirty feet before I lost my balance and ended up careening into a holly bush. Yeah, the ones with the sharp spikes on their leaves. By the time I climbed out of it, I was as awake as I'd been in days and determined not to be deterred by the momentary painful setback.

I remembered reading once that when you finally achieve balance, you never lose it, so I just needed to prove or disprove that statement for myself. Turns out, the statement was true. I did much better on my second try. Now, onward to discover more truths.

My next discovered truth was that I'm REALLY out of shape, as in wheezing out of control, with a sore butt and tired legs within the first few miles. Okay, within the first mile, so I pulled off the mountain road to take a swig from the bottle and get my bearings. Discovery number three stared me in the face in the form of an attractive sign in a gray and purple motif:

Unity Center of the Mountains

My little getaway community has a Unity Cult Center? Who would have thunk? I walked the bike down the dirt road that was just barely single lane and had to move off to the side a couple times to let cars pass. Of course, today was Sunday, so these must be stragglers heading home or on to a Sunday brunch somewhere. I tapped my back pocket to be sure I had my trusty pad and pen before proceeding, my journalistic instincts on red alert. *I smell a story,* I thought. *How this well-honed cult was methodically creeping into the very fabric of small town Amberica under the guise of a legitimate religion. Pulitzer Prize, here I come.*

Now, my only defense for such banal, delusional thinking was that I was still mostly drunk from the previous twenty-four hour binge, heightened by the rot gut that was now about half gone. To say I entered the sanctuary with a chip on my shoulder would be a gross understatement. That it was promptly knocked off by what I found inside probably surprises no one but me.

I found only three people still in the large room filled with chairs, not pews—a young couple who were clearly in love, from the fact that they were holding hands and glancing from time to time at each other and then to the third person. It was this third individual who grabbed most of my attention. She was tall, close to six feet I estimated. Being over six-feet myself, I find such women interesting, especially when they are as attractive as this one was. She wore large, black rimmed glasses, which blended well with her ebony black hair that she had tied in a single pony tail trailing down one shoulder. I estimated she was either in her late thirties or early forties, a little older than I normally find appealing, but I clearly was willing to make an exception in her case.

The young couple finished their conversation and turned to leave. I heard them both say, "Namaste," and the woman replied in kind. *Ahh, New Agers,* I thought. Of course. What had I expected?

I strolled on over and held out my hand. She smiled and took it, gripping it firmly, but without trying to prove her strength, unlike what most men did. I liked her immediately, and then berated myself for it. *Remember, you're a journalist on a hot story that could lead to a Pulitzer.* I know, delusional.

"Hello, I'm Brasten Gramarly," I said. "You may have seen my show on MSNBC."

She shook her head. "Sorry, I don't watch TV very often. I take it MSNBC is on television?"

"Are you kidding..." I started, then stopped. "Yes, that's right. Cable."

"I see. I'm Bree Taylor." She looked around. "I guess this is my form of cable."

"You run this place?" I asked.

"Well, no." She laughed. "I'm one of the ministers who serves our congregants here. God is the one in charge."

"Oh, right, of course." *Another New Age wackadoodle. Seems like I'm surrounded by them these days.* Still, I found myself oddly attracted to her. After all, I'm still a man and she was a good looking woman.

"Bree? That's interesting. Family name?"

"Yes, indirectly. I was named after my grandfather, Brian Taylor. Do you live around here?"

"No, well, not always. I have a place down the road I come to when I have to get out of the city."

She nodded. "I see. Well, feel free to attend any of our services when you're around. We have two on Sunday, one at 9 AM and the other starting at 11, and a Wednesday meditation from 7 to 9 PM."

"Good to know," I replied. *So, that's how they quietly recruit new members to their cult. Extend an innocent invitation.* My journalist's instincts were wide awake, but so also was my masculine curiosity to get to know Ms. Bree Taylor better.

"That's kind of you. I'll keep it in mind," I continued. "I'm really more of a candlelight dinner with a fine Bordeaux kind of guy. Maybe we could do dinner sometime, and you could tell me how you got into..." I almost said "this cult", but caught myself at the last moment, "...saving people's souls." I realized that probably sounded just as bad.

Bree chuckled, then cocked her head to one side. "Thanks, but no thanks."

"Really? Why? Am I too old for you?"

She studied me a moment before replying. "No, hardly. I'm sure you're very nice, and I bet you're good at showing the ladies a good time."

I nodded. "Yes, that's right."

"Unfortunately, you're too much of a bag of troubles. Tell you what. You get your life together, stop drinking, find or create some purpose, then come back and ask me again. We'll see."

She turned to leave. "You have a good day, Mr. Gramarly. Let yourself out when you're done. You might enjoy checking out our bookstore. If you see something you like, just put the money on the desk. Alicia will collect it in the morning." She pointed off to her left. "A lot of good wisdom for anyone ready to put their house in order."

I watched in amazement as she strolled away. I had just been royally put in my place, and while I hated to admit it, she was absolutely right. My life was a mess. It reminded me of an old joke by Groucho Marx about not wanting to be a member of any club that would have him as a member. I wouldn't want to date someone who was willing to go out with a person with my messed up life.

I peddled home with the proverbial tail between my legs and tossed the empty pint bottle in the trash can next to the kitchen door, ate an early supper and went to bed, where I tossed and turned most of the night with the question of how I was going to get my life in order haunting me. In the morning, I awoke to find a stack of books sitting next to the kitchen door with a note:

Thought you'd find these useful as you get your life in order.
Bree

I unwrapped the package and found six books, all by the same author—Angeline Tarkington. Was this an answer to my nightlong prayer or was it just God jabbing me in the ribs for the fun of it? I fixed myself a pot of coffee, then sat down and opened the first book. *Beggars can't be choosers,* I thought, as I began to read. Somewhere in the course of a day of reading and journaling, I called and left a message for Edward to please get someone to cover my show for the next few days, and I'd be in touch soon. Then I went back to reading.

On Wednesday, I peddled over to the Unity Center, but left my pad and pen at home. There might be a story there, but it wasn't about it being a cult, that much I was damn sure.

Angeline Responds

SO IT APPEARS WOO-WOO Woman Tarkington isn't such an angel after all. What do you expect from the Dems? No doubt one more candidate about to drop out of the race. Tweet by President Oscar Wellian

"YOU HAVE TO SCHEDULE a press conference," Stella pleaded, as she sat across from Angeline, her candidate. "This isn't going to go away. The Republicans and Wellian won't let it."

"Well, it's finally getting my name in the news," Angeline replied with a sheepish smile.

"Yeah, but that old saying that even negative publicity is good is so not true, and the more you refuse to comment, the more room you give the opposition to make up stories."

"Then I'll tell them that my personal life is out of bounds." Angeline stood up and started pacing.

"Sorry, no pass," Stella countered. I know you well enough that trying such a move would be out of integrity for you."

Angeline walked over and poured herself a drink of water before continuing to walk around the room, finally coming to a stop in front of her campaign manager. "So, what is in integrity for me, oh wise one?"

Stella smiled at the term. "Tell the truth...tell it succinctly, simply and quickly. "You have to come clean or your political career is over."

Angeline resumed walking for close to a minute before saying, "Okay, schedule a press conference for tomorrow morning, 9 AM."

Stella stood up, walked over and gave her a hug. "That's my girl."

The next morning, promptly at 9 AM, Angeline Tarkington walked out of her campaign headquarters to a line of microphones and clicking of cameras. She waited for a moment as she looked over the expectant crowd of reporters.

Stella had already prepared them that she'd be giving them a statement, but would not be taking questions at this time.

"I am not a perfect human being," she began, looking from side to side. "I have made my share of mistakes in the past, maybe more than my share. There have been times I have let people down. I've hurt people, a few quite badly." She paused and smiled. "And I have asked God and them to forgive me. As I just said, I am far from perfect, just like our forefathers who wrote the Declaration of Independence. They, too, were not perfect, yet they were able to write a declaration that created a country unlike anything ever seen or imagined. And while we as a country are also not perfect, tens of millions of people have been empowered and have had their lives enhanced by what those men wrote and for which they were willing to give their lives."

She paused again before smiling. "Thank you." She turned to leave as the reporters burst forth with questions. "What about the baby? Did you have a child out of wedlock? Are the allegations true..." She waved to the reporters and re-entered her headquarters.

"Now, let's get back to work," she said, as she passed Stella.

"But..." Stella started to say, then noticed the look of determination on Angeline's face. "Yes, ma'am."

IT DIDN'T TAKE LONG before I realized that getting my house in order wasn't as easy as it sounded, even though Angeline stressed that in her books. I did join an AA group when I returned to the city, but dropped out after a few meetings when I learned that you weren't supposed to date anyone for at least the first year. While I wasn't ready to start dating, I didn't like someone telling me I couldn't. What would happen if I met someone that I found really attractive, maybe someone even prettier and more intriguing than Bree Taylor?

And yes, I continued to think about her a lot, especially on nights when I so wanted to drop down to my local liquor store and buy a bottle. I had poured the bottles of booze I had in my apartment down the drain as one of my first acts while attending the AA meetings.

I found myself drawn to my mountain getaway more and more, leaving right after my Friday show, and staying until Monday morning. And yes, I biked to the Unity Center on Sundays after checking to see which service Bree would be the speaker for, but I sat in the back with a cap drawn over my face and left during the final song to avoid having to shake her hand as the rest of the congregation filed out. Over the next several weeks I found biking around the mountain roads easier and less painful, though I did finally have to break down and get a more comfortable seat.

The nights were the hardest, especially those in the city after my shows. During those times, I'd pull out one of the books Bree had given me and read a chapter or two, then journal about what I'd read as suggested in the first book. It helped, but the pull to climb back into a bottle was strong, no lie. But I didn't. I'm not sure why. I think a big part of it was I really did want to see what it would be like to go out with someone like Bree, and yes, I admit to having some flights of fancy about what she'd be like in bed, but tried to stay away from such thoughts. She deserved better than that.

Also, I noticed that the process was working. Slowly, painfully, but steadily, my life began to improve. Even my show ratings improved as I became more conscious of my guests and treated them with more respect, while maintaining a renewed interest in my journalistic integrity. Even Edward and Cynthia began to notice the change.

"Who is she?" Cynthia asked one morning when she caught me humming an unrecognizable tune as I sat at my desk.

"What? Who? What are you talking about?"

"There must be a woman in your life," she continued. "She's either a really good lay, or she's a saint. I'm not sure which."

"Don't be silly. I'm not sleeping with anyone," I objected.

"Than who is this saintly woman who's willing to put up with you? Now, don't get me wrong. I think it's great. She's doing wonders with you. So, who is she?"

I dropped the papers I'd been reading on my desk and leaned back in my chair. An image of Bree standing at the front of the sanctuary speaking to her flock flashed in my mind, but I shook it away. "Nope, you're completely off course on this one. I just realized that I need to make a few minor adjustments, that's all. I'm the master of my own ship, so I'm in control." *Damn, that's straight from the book I'm reading,* I realized.

"Don't you have something else to work on?" I decided it was high time to change the subject before I spouted out any more New Age aphorisms.

Cynthia eyed me suspiciously before shrugging. "Well, two more candidates have dropped out of the race. Is that what you mean?"

"Yes, exactly," I replied, relieved that my ploy had worked. "Was one of them Tarkington?"

"No," Cynthia snapped back defensively. "It's Hampton Connors and Amelia Chang, and not surprisingly, they both endorsed Senator O'Hare, or at least it sounds like they will in the next few days." She paused a moment as though considering whether to say what was on her mind. And then, of course, she did. "You know, it's those type of comments that drive me crazy. You just assumed she's going to drop out, but I can promise you this—she's not about to, despite being shunned by most of the mainstream media. She's in it all the way."

"Okay, okay. No need to get mad. I was just wondering. Her poll numbers remain low after that debacle with the mystery child."

"Which continues to be completely unfounded," Cynthia pointed out. "You know, she writes about being the captain of your own ship in one of her early books."

"Really? How curious," I replied. "And here I'm pretty sure I read it in a fortune cookie just the other night. Funny, it didn't appear to be a quote from her. Now, how about getting out of here so at least one of us can get some work done."

She turned to leave, but then stopped with one hand on the door knob. "You know, it's been several weeks since you've interviewed her. Maybe it's..."

"No can do," I interrupted her. "Remember what Edward heard from upstairs. That hasn't changed. Now, please." I pointed to the door, and she grudgingly left.

But she had planted a seed that found fertile ground in my psyche. For the rest of the day, I kept thinking about what I could do to help my newly adopted secret mentor. A plan started coming together.

A Second Seance

THE DEMS ARE SCRAMBLING to try to find someone in their party that can defeat me. What a futile effort. Candidates are dropping like flies. Tweet by President Oscar Wellian

ANOTHER CANDIDATE, Albert Homintash, dropped out less than a week later, claiming he was ending his bid because it was time for the Democratic Party to come together in the spirit of solidarity and a commitment to beating President Wellian, no matter what. He claimed such joining of forces was more important than his remaining in the race. Two days later the *New York Times* reported his campaign coffers were bare and conjectured that this had more to do with his dropping out. The following day, in an effort to prove such a hypothesis to be unfounded, Homintash scheduled a press conference, in which he proposed a Pledge of Solidarity.

"Everyone who's either still in this race or has dropped out needs to pledge that they will support and endorse whoever comes out the winner. Any one of us will do a better job than having President Wellian in the White House for four more years."

It took less than a week for all the other Democratic candidates to sign the pledge—all except Angeline Tarkington.

"Are you kidding me?!" I fairly shouted at Cynthia as she delivered the news. "Why on earth would she not sign the pledge? Surely she must realize she doesn't have a snowball's chance in hell to become the party's choice."

"Well, all I know is that she has had three interviews in the last twenty-four hours after refusing to sign," Cynthia retorted, then added, "She's not dumb, you know, and Stella, her campaign manager, is as savvy as they come."

"So, you think this is just a ploy to get her in front of the camera?" I asked. *If so, it was a pretty smart move and one that's working,* I thought.

"Well, it's working, isn't it?" Cynthia replied before dropping a stack of papers on my desk and sashaying out of the office.

Yes, it definitely is, I thought, as I pushed the stack to one side and made a mental note to return them to her the next day. Got to keep our little paper shuffling game alive, after all. I pulled out my trusty journalist's notepad and turned to the back where I had a list of bullet points that was becoming the framework of my plan. At the top of the first page was the title:

How to Dump Wellian and Elect A. T.

After adding the new idea, I read over the fifteen or twenty other ones. *It's coming together quite nicely,* I thought. *This just might work.*

I could have sworn I heard in the background of my mind Dottie's voice. *You're damn right it will. Keep it up, big boy. I'm proud of you.*

I closed the notebook and stuck it back in my pocket, then stood up. I rode the elevator down to the ground floor to go to lunch. Today being Thursday, that meant a blackened chicken salad at Freddie's. Not necessarily the best or closest restaurant for such a meal, but one that was precisely five miles away. I walked outside and unlocked the chain on my second bike I'd recently purchased, and put on my helmet. Riding in downtown New York City might still be my own attempt at suicide, but I was committed to taking off at least another ten pounds and biking was an integral part of the plan. Of course, the greater plan was to win over Bree Taylor, come hell or high water.

OVER THE NEXT FEW DAYS, my plan fell in place and now all there was to do was to implement it and be ready to make adjustments as needed, like any other plan. The ultimate objective was clear even though there were two pathways I could see to it.

Plan one was to help Angeline Tarkington become the next President of the United States, which would so impress Bree when I shared how I'd orchestrated it that she'd fall head over heels for me. Now being a believer in visualization from one of Tarkington's book, I imagined her falling into my arms once I shared my account of my own personal role in the victory. At the same time, being a practical sort of guy, I had an alternate plan just in case.

In this scenario, Tarkington would fail to win, but in the process of trying to make it happen, I would have gotten myself and my life in such shape that once again, Bree would fall for me. So, the end result would be the same for me, although the country would end up suffering greatly.

I had one main operating principle that I was adamant not to violate. Being committed to a certain level of journalistic integrity, my main objective was to be sure Angeline had sufficient opportunities to share with the public her views and positions, something that the mainstream media seemed to be set against. I would not try to influence either what she said or how the public responded.

It was time for me to start redeeming the bounty of favor chips I'd accumulated over the past twenty years. I prayed that they would be enough.

IT DIDN'T MAKE SENSE to Angeline why her Inner Guidance had given her such a clear sign to take the action she was contemplating, but despite trying to ignore or rationalize that guidance away, she could no longer ignore it. Over the years, she'd learned to trust that guidance, especially when it was as insistent as it was this time.

So, she took a couple days off to return to her home to perform the ritual as she'd been instructed. Being home always felt good, especially after being away for so long. The sunroom she entered was one of her favorite places. She used it for rest and rejuvenation, as well as when she was called to this special task.

Once again, she wore her favorite prayer shawl and went through the identical breathing exercises to quiet her mind. This time she added an additional prayer that this trip to another's world wouldn't be so painful or take so long from which to recover. As before, after a few minutes of preparation, she removed a set of photos from her pocket and laid them on the altar. She studied each one, trying to discern why in the world she had been guided to enter this man's world. It made no sense. She'd had little contact with him, especially since his industry had apparently put out the word to ignore her.

Trust the process, she heard once again from her Inner Guidance. She smiled and took a few more deep, cleansing breaths before letting her eyes lose focus as she slipped into Brasten Gramarly's world.

It Hits the Fan

THE ECONOMY IS BOOMING, the stock market is soaring, and all is right with the world as we prepare to run the country for four more years. Tweet by President Oscar Wellian

IN HINDSIGHT, IT WAS inevitable that there would be a major catastrophe at least once during the campaign period, given how long the election cycle is these days and how many disasters we seem to face as a nation.

But, really, did it have to be another mass shooting, especially one of such magnitude?

45 Gunned Down in Latest Mass Shooting
Dozens More Injured

I groaned as I sat at the kitchen table munching on my toast and drinking coffee. The news cycle would be filled for days with various accounts of the incident that happened in St. Louis late the previous evening, as a shooter placed himself on a nearby roof with an AK-47 style assault rifle and gunned down teenagers and young adults as they exited from a rock concert.

He had eventually turned one of his guns on himself as the SWAT team closed in on him, but not before achieving notoriety for pulling off one of the most gruesome mass shootings in history.

I knew the drill. Hell, we all did. We'd been through it so often. There would be a prayer vigil spontaneously set up somewhere close to the site of the shooting with hundreds or even thousands of grieving citizens migrating to pay their respects. And, of course, there'd be the same old rhetoric about how we really needed to do something this time, with the other side saying how awful it was for the Liberals to try to politicize such a tragic event.

The NRA would claim once again that people killed people, not guns, and that background checks weren't the answer...on and on and on. By the time I got into work, several of the remaining candidates had released statements condemning and consoling. They all agreed that we needed to do something this time, and offered their own ideas what that something should be.

The only one who didn't release a statement was Angeline Tarkington. Instead, she called a press conference to be held later that day at the scene of the tragedy.

"Well, that's ballsy," I said, when Cynthia came in to deliver the news.

"I'll say," she agreed. "Want to watch it with me? It's at three o'clock."

"Sure." *Why not*, I thought. Probably just be the same ol' same ol', but I didn't have anything else scheduled for the afternoon.

I arrived a few minutes late to the lounge where several other staff members had congregated to hear what Tarkington had to say. Cynthia motioned to me that she'd saved me a seat up close. I wound my way through the others, excusing myself for interrupting things.

"...Perhaps it is time we look beyond just the symptoms and look deeper to the root cause of acts as heinous as those of yesterday evening. Mass shootings have become all too commonplace in this country," Tarkington said, as she looked out over the crowd that had gathered. "They are just the bloody tip of a much greater iceberg. They are not even the number one cause of death by firearms. No, my friends. Suicide is. Sixty percent of all firearm deaths are self-inflicted, and no, these are not accidents."

She paused and wiped the tears from her eyes. "There is a pervasive sickness of despair and resignation permeating through our country, but even these are only symptoms. What is the cause?"

She paused again. "I assert it is that we are a country of souls being governed by the soulless. Please, may we take a moment to pray..."

NOT SURPRISINGLY, THE *New York Times* headline the following day was:

Candidate Tarkington Accuses President Wellian of Being Soulless

"Well, she's sure getting some media coverage now," I said, as Cynthia showed me the paper, even though she knew that the *Times* was in my newspaper stack.

"She's just doing what her campaign manager recommended she do," Cynthia replied. "She's telling her truth, pure and simple."

I stared long and hard at my assistant. "And how would you know what Stella told her to do?"

Cynthia smiled like a cat who'd just swallowed a canary. "Oh, I have my ways," was all she said.

"Don't tell me you have someone on the inside of Tarkington's campaign headquarters."

"Maybe..." she replied coyly. "What do you think about her comment?"

"That our esteemed POTUS has no soul?" I asked. "I don't know, it seems pretty obvious to me if you look at his draconian policies, but it feels a little bit like pointing out to the emperor that he's wearing no clothes. It might be true, but that doesn't mean it isn't also dangerous to point it out."

"Whatever happened to the person who pointed out that the emperor was naked?" Cynthia asked.

"Hmm, I don't have the foggiest idea. I'm not really into reading fairy tales these days. Why don't you get Bridgette on the research team to look into it. They don't seem to be doing much else these days."

"I might just do that, but I'll Google it first." She turned and walked out of the office.

She reported to me later that her research revealed it took an innocent child to point out the obvious nakedness of the emperor, but she wasn't sure what happened to the kid. *Probably went into politics,* I thought, *or rolled the simple truth into a reality TV show.*

Debate #3 Prep

WOO-WOO WITCH TARKINGTON has stepped over the line accusing me of not having a soul. Lucky for her she hasn't a chance of winning the Dem's nomination. I'd eat her alive. Tweet by President Oscar Wellian

WITH JUST A FEW DAYS remaining before the third debate, there were six candidates who had clearly made the higher criteria set by the DNC and three others, including Angeline Tarkington, that were still in question. That's when Tarkington once again called a press conference. *That's it for her,* I thought, as I weaved in and out of traffic on my bike. *This will break Cynthia's heart.* I decided to stop at the bakery a few doors down from the studio to pick up a couple of her favorite pastries to help soften the blow.

We all convened in the viewing room to hear Tarkington's exit speech. Bridgette sat with Cynthia, a box of tissues between them.

"Thank you for coming today," Angeline said, as she gazed over the crowd of reporters with a charming smile on her face. *She seems awfully calm, considering what she's about to announce.* I glanced over to Cynthia, who looked like she was just barely holding it together. *Poor girl. I wonder which candidate she'll get behind now.*

"We're just a few days out from our next debate, and I want to thank all the people who have stepped up and contributed to my campaign. For the past couple of days, I've been meeting with my staff, as well as checking in with my Inner Guidance. I've been told that we still have a mathematical chance to make the cutoff, but...," she paused and surveyed the crowd, "...I've decided to withdraw from the race."

There was a rash of camera clicks, and then the questions started to fly. "What made you decide to withdraw from the race to be the Democratic candidate to run against President Wellian?" the most vocal reporter asked the question everyone else wanted the answer to.

Tarkington held up her hand for silence and when she got it, she shook her head. "I'm sorry. You misunderstood what I meant. I'm not withdrawing from that race. No, I'm still in it, and I'm in it to win it. I'm withdrawing from the race to be in this next debate." There was a rumbling of whispers and comments, hushed once more by Tarkington. "Listen, the DNC has every right to decide who will participate in their debates. However, I would suggest to them they consider coming up with a new name for their party since the way they're going about it is far from democratic."

"What do you mean by that?" one of the reporters asked.

"Well, for example. The latest debate standard uses polling as a criterion, but most of those polls only call people with landlines. That's not a representative sample of the nation's demographics. There are millions of citizens nowadays who only have a cellphone, with a high percentage of those being younger people."

"Now, I know it's going to be a bit harder becoming the Democratic Party's nominee if I'm not on that debate stage in a few days, especially with my calling out the DNC in this way. So be it. We'll just find some other way to get our message out to the citizens of this country, and I have no question that, with the guidance of the Almighty, we will. Thank you for your attention."

Are you kidding me?! I thought, but managed to keep from shouting it. Cynthia and Bridgette jumped up and down and gave each other high-fives, while everyone else looked at each other with stunned looks on their faces. I turned to Edward, who was sitting next to me. "Sounds like political suicide to me. What do you think?"

Edward shrugged. "I don't know. It's gutsy. I'll give her that." He leaned over close to me and said in a much softer voice meant for my ears only. "You know, Arnie left for a two week vacation in the Alaska wilderness where he won't have any contact with civilization, not even cellphone coverage."

"Yeah?" I asked, curious why he would share such information with me. "So?"

"So, it might be time to have Ms. Tarkington back on your show. What do you say?"

It was my turn to give him a high-five. "Excellent idea. Make it so!"

And he did. Two nights later, Angeline came onto my show with more surprising information, but before that, more breaking news hit the airwaves the following day.

THE NEXT DAY, THE *Washington Post* ran an exclusive story chronicling the infidelities of Senator Reginald O'Hare, complete with photographs and eye witness accounts from over half a dozen men and women who'd known about his sexual proclivities and had previously either chosen to look the other way or had been paid to keep their mouths shut. By noon, the O'Hare campaign had released a statement that Senator O'Hare had taken ill and would need to withdraw from the race to run against President Wellian and would be taking a leave of absence from the Senate as well.

"Holy smoke!" I shouted, as I entered the network offices. *Are you kidding me?* just didn't seem strong enough this go around.

"Yeah, I know," Edward replied, in his customarily understated way. "This throws the whole race up for grabs, and it makes the debate next week that much more important."

"I'll say. Do you think our guest tomorrow night might reconsider her decision to withdraw from it?"

"Well, you'll have a chance to ask her just that," Edward replied, folding the paper and tossing it on the stack of other newspapers. "While she was a long shot to actually qualify, with the frontrunner out, who knows what the polls might reflect at this point. I would think they'd have to consider the more recent polls, especially those that come in after this news."

"Who would you say the new frontrunner will be?"

Edward shook his head and shrugged at the same time. "It's anyone's guess at this point."

Social Media

WASN'T IT O'HARE THAT led the charge against me when I was falsely accused of sleeping around? Wow! Now that's a perfect case of the pot calling the kettle black. RIP O'Hare. Tweet by President Oscar Wellian

---

"LET'S WELCOME OUR NEXT guest, one of the Democratic candidates still in the race, who, according to her own words, is 'in it to win it', Angeline Tarkington. Welcome to The Brass Brasten Show, candidate Tarkington."

"It's a pleasure," Angeline said, as she shook my hand across the table. "Before we start, might we just take a moment of silent prayer for Senator O'Hare and his family during this most trying of times?" She shut her eyes before I could say anything, so I squinted mine almost closed as well, while Edward shouted in my ear about 'dead air time.' After about fifteen seconds, she opened her eyes and smiled at the camera. "Thank you." She turned to me and nodded.

"Well, certainly with this latest turn of events, I'm sure everyone is wondering if you're reconsidering your decision to not try to qualify for next week's debate."

"Oh, no," Angeline replied. "My staff would like me to, and sure made their opinions heard, quite loudly I might add, but after thoughtful meditation and prayer, my guidance is clear. Plus, we have a plan already that I believe will serve quite nicely."

"Really?" I said. "Would you care to share it here on national television or is it a secret between you and your 'Inner Guide?'"

Angeline chuckled. "Oh, no, it's not a secret. I'm only too happy to share it with you and your audience. It's really quite simple. I'm going to have my own debate."

My mouth must have dropped open by that comment for my guest smiled at me reassuringly. "You're what?"

"Well, the debate is next Tuesday, right?"

"Yes, that's right, and we'll be covering it right here on this network," I added before Edward could shout in my ear again.

"So, by the end of the evening, everyone will know the questions that were asked. On Wednesday, I'm going to have my own live event on Facebook. By midnight Tuesday, we'll have posted on AngelineTarkingtonforpresident.com[1] a survey with the list of questions. People can vote which questions they'd most want me to address, and...," she paused again for emphasis, "...suggest five other questions not asked in the debate they want me to answer. For me, that's democracy in action in the twenty-first century."

That's brilliant, I thought, as I slowly closed my mouth and tried to remain somewhat neutral. "That's an interesting idea."

"Thank you, and that's not all."

"There's more?"

"Oh, yes. I'm also going to invite any of the other candidates who'd like to come and be a part of it. While we won't have time to have them all answer each of the questions, I'll give them the opportunity to answer the top two questions the citizens of this great nation choose. It should be a lot of fun."

"Yes, indeed it should," I replied.

"Oh, and one other thing. As you know, I have many wonderful men and women of all ages and all different walks of life who are very supportive of what we're doing. We're asking all of them who are on social media to please share our debate with their friends and family members. Over this next week, I suspect there will be many hundreds of thousands of people who are able to hear our message of Divine Love, compassion and kindness, and how they can overcome the fear and hate that have been rampant during the Wellian administration."

I turned to the camera as I said, "Well, I believe we made some news tonight." I turned back to my guest. "Thank you for coming on the show and sharing your plan with us. I'm sure many people are looking forward to your post debate debate."

I turned back to the second camera. "Are you kidding me? I'm pretty sure our guest tonight is very serious, so watch this space. Good night."

---

1.   http://angelinetarkingtonforpresident.com/

I WOULD HAVE THOUGHT, given the bombshell news that Tarkington delivered on my show, that my talk show colleagues on the other networks would have picked it up and run with it, at least including it in the news spot about the upcoming debate, but all I heard was crickets when it came to her strategy and plans to hold her own debate. Well, crickets were prevalent on the other networks, but for sure Tarkington's Angels had picked up on her challenge and were lighting the social media channels on fire.

So, now we're going to have a division between mainstream media and social media? I wondered as I put my cellphone in my pocket and headed downstairs to go to work. It sure looked like it. Mainstream media was itself divided, with clear lines between conservative coverage and more moderate, or even liberal, news. If you didn't like either of those, you could check in on Facebook, or Twitter, or Instagram, or...the list goes on.

Since my network was an integral part of the mainstream media, we focused primarily on the upcoming debate, but I did encourage the other talk show hosts to at least mention Tarkington's upcoming Facebook Live event. Some did, but most of them ignored my suggestion. It was beginning to feel like, short of calling in my favors and, in some cases, resorting to extortion or blackmail, Tarkington's message would be relegated to just social media.

This began to shift when three of the former candidates who'd dropped out of the race accepted Angeline's invitation to be a part of her debate, followed shortly thereafter by one of the current candidates accepting as well. Now, the networks had to include at least a mention of her plan. Of course, CBS, who was hosting the debate, loved the extra attention, which meant more viewers and a higher rating.

Turned out that the third debate was flat by most reviewers' accounts, including my own. By now, the field had been cut down to the more conventional politicians, with each of them vying for as much time in front of the camera as possible. The clear winners on this particular night were the two remaining Senators, Barry Schneider of Vermont and Eloise Walker of Connecticut, with Vernon Johnson, the Governor of Colorado coming in a distant third. Walker and Schneider seemed to take turns agreeing that Wellian needed to be defeated no matter what, and then arguing with each other that they had the best chance to carry the Democratic Party across the finish line.

I found myself having trouble staying awake and, according to the ratings the next day, so did a lot of other people. One newspaper even called the winner of the third debate to be all the candidates who didn't make it on the stage, though I found that to be a bit cynical even for my taste. So, the stage was set for Angeline Tarkington's Facebook Live debate the following evening.

The Chicago Os

ONCE AGAIN THE DEMS passed out massive doses of sleep aid to the Amberican public in the form of their third debate. How many more times will they abuse our people with such overdoses of drivel? Tweet by President Oscar Wellian

NOT SURPRISINGLY, TARKINGTON'S Facebook Live event ran into a few early technical glitches as hundreds of thousands of curious citizens tried to log in from around the country at the same time. However, the Tarkington campaign had anticipated that might happen and was able to work with Facebook headquarters to get the matter resolved in less than fifteen minutes.

It turned out that Governor Vernon Johnson, who'd been part of the previous night's debate and had accepted Tarkington's invitation to join hers, had bowed out at the last minute, claiming illness and fatigue. That left Hampton Connors, Amelia Chang and Albert Homintash as her guests, but truthfully, they would have been smarter to take Johnson's strategy and stay home for it was Angeline's night all the way with thousands of people leaving comments for her throughout the evening.

Perhaps the highlight of the night was the last question, which had not been part of Tuesday's debate, but had been an overwhelming favorite of people filling out the survey. So popular was the question that Tarkington invited the other three candidates to respond to it as well: "What makes you the candidate most likely to be able to beat Wellian in November?"

The three candidates took their turns responding to the question, outlining their various plans for bringing the country back on course, but without directly answering the question, as all good politicians learned in Politics 101. Then it was Tarkington's turn.

"I want to first thank my fellow candidates for joining me tonight to demonstrate what politics can be like in this twenty-first century." She nodded to each of them. "Now, as to the question of beating Wellian...if you think simply having a lot of plans and strategies is what will win in November, we're in trouble. President Wellian has a solid base of voters who are ready to come out in droves to see that he remains in office for another term. No, we must have a major shift in the consciousness of our citizens away from the attitude of fear and hate that has been so rampant since even before Wellian took office, and that he has fostered for the last three-plus years."

She paused and took a drink of water before turning back to the camera. "I have devoted my life to people's personal development and transformation, and that's why I am the candidate who will win in November, for the shift in consciousness back to a moral, conscience-driven country starts with each of us. Gandhi said it best many years ago—'Be the change you want to see in the world.' I am prepared to lead this country back to such a mindset and awareness, and with your help, we will set this country back on course, and then these plans and strategies so aptly outlined by my colleagues here tonight will work." She smiled into the camera and placed one hand over her heart before continuing.

"Thank you all for sharing this special time with me this evening. Please help us share our message of Universal Love, compassion and kindness by inviting your friends, family and business associates to view the recording of this event over the next week. And I look forward to seeing many of you in Chicago in a few months for the Democratic National Convention. Good night."

"MISS O, YOUR GUESTS have arrived. I showed them to the study as you requested."

"Thank you, Meg. I'll be right there." The statuesque black woman looked up from the journal in which she'd been writing. "How are you today?"

Meg smiled. It had become their morning routine whenever they first met. "I'm good, Miss O. One day at a time." She fought to keep her eyes from darting to her left arm, where the needle tracks were still visible.

"That's good, my dear. One day at a time for all of us." She stood up, placing the journal in the nightstand drawer next to her bed before walking over to the large windows that looked out on the rolling hills of her estate. Even though she'd been writing about today's meeting with her two friends, she took a moment longer for a few deep breaths as she recited the last lines she'd written in her journal. "Committed and unattached, trusting the Divine knows best."

She turned to smile at her assistant. "Let's do this." She squared her shoulders and strode out of the room and to the study.

As she entered the spacious room, three of its four walls lined with books, she held out her arms and felt the joy in her heart at seeing the tall, lanky black man come towards her with his arms outstretched as well, followed closely behind by his beautiful wife. "It's been too long," Miss O said as they hugged, then turned to hug the other woman as well.

"I know, but it's inevitable, given these changing times, that the 'Chicago O's' would have to slow down long enough to spend a little time together."

"'The Chicago O's'. I like that. Please sit. Thank you so much for accepting my invitation. You both look well. Life after the White House must agree with you."

Her two guests looked at each other and nodded, before the man replied. "Yes, and no. We don't miss the constant pressure that comes with the position, but I think I can speak for both of us in saying that we're distressed by these last three years. It's become far worse than either of us could have imagined."

Miss O nodded. "I understand completely, which is why I asked you here today. I believe it's paramount that we all do what we can to begin to right the ship, starting with this next election." She paused to take a deep breath. "That's why I plan to come out for one of the candidates in the near future."

Her two guests stared first at her and then at each other. "And who would that be?" the woman asked. "Are you at liberty to say?"

"Yes, it's Angeline Tarkington." Miss O paused to study their reactions, and was a bit surprised that they weren't more shocked. *Unless they learned from their years in politics to hide such reaction,* she thought. She let another few seconds elapse before she added, "And I am hoping you might support her as well." *Ahh, now there's the reaction I was expecting.*

The man stood up and started pacing, studying the books along one wall. Finally, he turned and asked, "And what might such support look like? You know, as a former President, I must be very careful in such matters."

"Yes, I realize that," Miss O replied. "And that's why I wanted us to meet and work out our strategy. I think we can all agree that any of the candidates now running would do a far better job than our current President. Agreed?"

Her two guests nodded. "For sure," the woman added.

"And yet, I don't believe we need to settle for just better, and I for one am not willing to compromise when it comes to the wellbeing of our country. I think we need to go all the way to a major transformation, one that will reverberate from sea to shining sea and beyond, to the rest of the world."

"Eloquently said, as always," the man replied. "And do you have a plan for this global transformation?"

Miss O smiled. "You know I do. Would you like to hear it?"

The man and woman both nodded.

"Great," Miss O said, as she stood up and walked over to the large mahogany desk at the far end of the room. "Please, step into my peace room."

Two hours later, Miss O looked up from the papers on the desk. "So, are we aligned? I'll take care of reaching out to the public and pooling the power of our citizens together, and you'll manage the political arena?"

The husband and wife glanced at each other before he replied, "Yes, that's agreeable. Do you know how you'll go about bringing our diverse population together?"

"Well, not completely, but much of the plan has come to me through Spirit. I know two young people that I plan to enroll into helping me who I believe will be only too happy to assist, and if so, will make my part much easier. And you? What's the next step for your role?"

"Well, I think Millicent and I need to start working behind the scenes by contacting the candidates who are no longer in the running and see who we can bring onto the team. It seems ironic that this year's Democratic National Convention will be right here in Chicago. I only pray that history not repeat itself."

"I agree," Miss O said, as she reached out and shook his hand, then gave him and his wife a big hug. "We'll stay in close communication in the coming weeks. Could we end our time together today with a moment of silent prayer?"

The three of them came together in a tight circle and bowed their heads. After a minute or two, the three opened their eyes and Miss O declared, "Game On."

After Meg showed their guests out, she returned to see what was next on her boss's agenda. "How about getting Queen B on the line. I texted her last night, so she should be expecting my call."

"Yes, ma'am. And after that?"

Miss O glanced at her diamond-studded watch. "I should have time to call T. S., then we'll break for lunch." *And that should make for a very good first half of the day.*

The Democratic Convention Approaches

IF YOU THOUGHT THE Dem's debates were boring (and I did), just wait until you see their Convention. On second thought, don't bother. Nothing to see. Tweet by President Oscar Wellian

A WEEK AND A HALF BEFORE the Democrats were to meet in Chicago for their national convention, there were still three candidates who had a mathematical chance to become their candidate of choice to run against the incumbent President. Much to everyone's ongoing amazement, Angeline Tarkington remained in the race, even though she was a distant third, with just enough delegates to keep the other two candidates, Senator Barry Schneider of Vermont and former Governor Eloise Walker of Connecticut, from winning the nomination. As each day went by, it looked more likely that it would be a contested convention.

"When was the last time we had such a convention?" I muttered to myself.

"The last one I know of was after Jeb Barkley had finished his two terms as President and that cute Jimmy Smits, the underdog, eventually beat out the other two candidates."

I smiled as I recognized Dottie's voice, then glanced at the kitchen cabinet where I'd routinely kept my stash of booze just to make sure I hadn't unknowingly slipped back into drinking. No, everything was just as it was supposed to be. So, why had Dottie reappeared? I turned in the direction of her voice to see her sitting on the corner of the faux granite countertop, her legs dangling over the edge just like I'd seen her do countless times before.

"What are you talking about, and by the way, where the hell have you been?"

"I'm talking about the last Democratic brokered convention," Dottie replied. "It was on *West Wing*. You remember. It was your favorite show, and you made me watch it over and over."

"You only watched the entire series once or twice," I countered. "I had to watch it the other four or five times on my own."

"As to where have I been..." Dottie continued. "You seemed to be doing pretty well on your own, so I thought I'd give you a little room."

"And now?"

She smiled. "I missed you."

And in that instant my heart melted once again. Man, how I missed her as well. I shook myself in an effort to not grow too maudlin. "Well, I missed you, too. Care for some coffee or a bagel?"

"Nah, not much into eating these days."

"So, besides the fantasy brokered convention on *West Wing*, when was the last real one we had, particularly of the Democratic Party? I mean, the Republicans' Convention was darn close to one, but eventually settled on Wellian as their candidate. But I can't remember when the Democrats last had one."

Dottie didn't answer for several seconds, but cocked her head to one side as though trying to come up with the answer. Finally, she nodded. "1952," she replied.

"Really, that far back? Are you sure?"

"Sure, I'm sure. It says so right on the Internet."

"Now, hold on just a minute. Don't tell me you have instant access to everything on the World Wide Web?"

"No, not instantaneous, but pretty darn close."

"Now, that's way cool." *Almost worth dying for,* I started to say, then thought better of it. "So, 1952," I said instead. "Wow, that was a long time ago."

Dottie cocked her head in the other direction before continuing. "Yes, before our time, but evidently it was quite a battle. Adlai Stevenson eventually won on the third ballot, even though at the start of the convention he insisted he was not a candidate."

Smart move, I thought. "Sounds like he played political possum until the right moment."

Dottie shrugged. "I wouldn't know. It was years before I was born."

"Yeah, me to," I agreed. "So, can you look into your crystal ball and tell me what happens at the convention? I could make some real jack with information like that."

Dottie shook her head as she jumped down from the countertop and walked over to me. "No can do. Besides, what would be the fun in that?"

"Making several thousand dollars betting on naming the winner sounds like great fun."

"No. I'm afraid you'll just have to keep doing what you're doing and see how it plays out." She reached over from behind me and gave me a hug. "But I want you to know how proud I am of what you're doing. There may still be a chance we'll be together again if you keep playing your cards right."

I leaned back in my chair and imagined her real arms around me, as I drew in a whiff of her perfume. My heart ached more in that moment than I could recall since her death. Finally, she released her grip on me and patted me on the shoulders with her hands. "But I will tell you that Ms. Tarkington has some good friends coming to her aid. It's going to be an interesting few days leading up to the convention."

I turned to see the look on her face to see if she was serious or just pulling my leg, but she was already gone.

NEEDLESS TO SAY, MS. O's announcement sent shock waves throughout the mainstream media, so strongly that even those stations who'd intentionally overlooked Angeline Tarkington's campaign couldn't completely ignore it now, though they tried to underplay the effect such an endorsement was likely to have. Until Angeline held a press conference late that afternoon.

"While I thank my dear friend for her kind words and for believing in me...." She paused before continuing. "Here's the thing. We all need to think and feel for ourselves. Sure, listen to what others have to say. Keep an open mind and heart and then trust your own inner guidance. You've heard me speak. You know what I stand for.." She paused again and smiled, glancing quickly to someone off camera. "If not, go to TarkingtonforPOTUS.com[1]. Listen and trust. If there's resonance in your heart, take action. Get involved. Let

---

1.   http://tarkingtonforpotus.com/

me repeat that. Get involved. The day of passive patriotism is dead, and if we collectively don't get off our couches and get involved, our country will die as well. Thank you."

Then she walked off the stage and didn't take any questions from the press. I think that's when I let go of any last remnants of cynicism or doubt. This woman needed to become the next President of Amberica. The question still remained—how?

A Week to Go

THE DEMS ARE HOPELESSLY trying to find someone in their party that can defeat me. So silly. Resistance is futile. I look forward to being your President for four more years. Tweet by President Oscar Wellian

WITH ONLY A WEEK TO go before the Democrats were due to meet in Chicago to nominate their candidate to run against Wellian, there was still no obvious choice with enough delegates to carry them over the finish line. Senator Schneider and former Governor Eloise Walker were neck and neck, each with between thirty-eight and forty percent of the delegates. Angeline Tarkington had about half of that.

Every time someone would ask her when she was going to withdraw from the race, she would only smile and say, "You know, God works in mysterious ways, and so far, She hasn't given me a clear sign that She wants me to withdraw. Until She does, I'm still in it to win it."

Then, a rumor started circulating that something was amiss among the Democratic Party's big wigs, so I arranged a clandestine meeting with my version of "Deep Throat", who had on a few other occasions given me useful intel.

We met at our customary location, a swanky bar in Manhattan, the polar opposite of The Dive. After a couple of drinks and catching up on our favorite sports teams, I approached the subject. "I hear there's some division in the Party. You know anything about it?"

DT stared into his Manhattan, then slowly nodded.

Trying to draw him out, I said, "But, then again, we're talking about the Democratic Party, right? When was the last time they demonstrated having their act together?"

My source nodded. "Yeah, true enough." He took a swig from his drink before continuing. "This time is different though."

I felt my heartbeat pick up just a bit, but managed to keep my mouth shut. Instead, I just continued to sip on my drink for a minute or two.

Finally, thinking he needed some prodding, I asked, "How so?"

"From what I hear, one of the Party's most influential members is causing a ruckus."

"Really? Tell me more."

He slowly shook his head in time with the rotating of the ice in his glass. "I better not."

I caught the bartender's eye and ordered another round of drinks. I didn't bother telling my friend that he was drinking doubles while mine were club soda. When the drinks had arrived and the bartender had returned to his neutral corner, I asked again.

"Well, do you know who this wave-maker is?"

He nodded.

"Would I recognize his name?" I hated playing the twenty question game, but also knew it could be effective at times like this.

"Oh, yeah. No question about it."

I don't know where the next question came from, but over the years I'd learned to trust my instincts on such matters. "He wouldn't be someone local to where the convention is being held, would he?"

"Who said it was a he?" My friend smiled demurely.

"Touché." I smiled back and just barely restrained from reaching out and grabbing him by the throat. "Well?"

"Well, what?"

I took another deep breath and imagined his eyes popping out of his head. "Well, is this man or woman whose name I would recognize from the Chicago area?"

He stared into his drink again before finally answering. "Yeah. How did you know? Who else have you been talking to?"

"You know I never reveal my sources. I value our relationship too much to ever do anything like that." I patted him on the back, maybe a little harder than necessary.

Another minute or two elapsed while we pretended to watch the football game on one of the wide screen TVs. "Any idea what this person is saying or doing that's causing such a stir?"

"Listen, what I'm about to say is off the record, and you didn't hear it from me. Got it?"

I nodded, then held my breath.

"The scuttlebutt is that h..." It almost sounded like my friend had said 'he' but I couldn't be sure. "...this person is going around asking some of the other candidates who have dropped out of the race to be ready to support a particular candidate who's still in."

Wow, now that would be newsworthy, I thought. "And would this person have the kind of clout that might sway some of these other candidates?"

My friend turned his attention back to his drink, picked it up and downed it, before swinging around in his chair. As he rose to leave, he replied. "Oh, yeah."

Ms. O & Friends

THE FIRST LADY AND I are considering a major refurbishing of the White House with a gold color scheme. After all, we want to be comfortable during our next four years. Tweet by President Oscar Wellian

THREE DAYS LATER AND with only a week to go before the start of the Democratic Convention, I was munching on a turkey on rye sandwich at my desk and catching up on some paperwork when Cynthia burst into my office.

I started to point to the intercom and suggest she try using it, but then stopped when I saw the look on her face. She raced around my desk and turned on the television sitting on the credenza behind me. I rarely used it, preferring to receive my news either from my phone or my morning papers, but I let her continue her mission.

As the TV screen came alive, Cynthia turned to me. "You won't eff-ing believe what's about to happen."

"What? Did Tarkington finally come to her senses and bow out?" I regretted saying it the instant it leapt out of my mouth, and I saw the flash of anger on my assistant's face, but it was gone as quickly as it appeared. "Oh, no, just the opposite." She pointed to the screen as she grabbed the remote and turned up the sound.

I watched as a large black lady stepped up to a row of mikes and raised her hands to quiet the crowd. Even though it had been years since I'd seen the woman, I instantly recognized her, as I'm sure millions of other viewers did as well.

"Why, that's Ms. O, isn't it? I thought she'd retired from making public appearances," I said.

"She had, which makes this just that much more amazing," Cynthia replied. "Now, hush. I want to hear what she's about to say."

We both turned our attention to the television. After a few more seconds, the crowd quieted down, and Ms. O lowered her hands. "Thank you for allowing me to speak to you today on such short notice. I have a brief announcement to make and then I'll turn the mics over to a couple of my good friends, who will share their news as well."

She paused and looked over the crowd, a mixture of news people and the general public that had apparently magically appeared when Ms. O released a press notice that she had some important news to share.

"My fellow citizens, and that includes you of the press as well, we are in some of the most turbulent times in our recent history. Not since the late sixties has there been such turmoil and divisiveness. This next election is not only an important moment in our nation's history, but one of the most important moments in all of human history."

She paused again, and surveyed the crowd. "Which is why I'm coming out of retirement to make this announcement today. I can no longer stand on the sidelines and simply pray for salvation from the dark forces that have gripped this country. No, I must do my part to help right the course of this fine nation, and it's for this reason that I am announcing today my endorsement of Angeline Tarkington to become our next President of the United States of Amberica."

A flurry of camera clicks ensued as new pictures were taken of the woman who had in her time been one of the most photographed of all people. She raised one hand and waited for the rumbling from the crowd to stop before continuing.

"As many of you know, Angeline and I go way back. We are not only professional colleagues, but also have become close friends, and yet..." She raised her hand again to quiet the crowd. "...and yet, it is not because of friendship that I am endorsing her. If anything, it was our friendship that kept me from speaking up before now. No, I am endorsing Ms. Tarkington because I know to the very soul of my being, she is the candidate that will lead us back to a moral, kind and compassionate country, and who will beat President Wellian in November!'

The crowd, which had now grown to several hundred, cheered, drowning out the questions from the news reporters. After several seconds, Ms. O raised her hands again and the crowd slowly grew silent.

"Now, I'd like to introduce a couple other dear friends, who will make their own announcements. Please, Queen B and T. S. Will you join me at the podium?" Now the crowd exploded, led in large part by the younger people, who'd somehow gotten word that two of their favorite singers and entertainers might just be there today.

Queen B and T. S. sashayed on stage, waving to the crowd, and stood on either side of Ms. O. After close to a minute of loud cheering, she grabbed a hand of each of them and raised them over their heads. The crowd yelled and screamed more loudly.

As the cheering continued, I turned to Cynthia. "This could be a game changer," I said.

"No shit," Cynthia replied. "This *is* a game changer. Chicago, here we come!"

The Dems Convention

NOW THE DEMS ARE CALLING upon old has beens and two never weres in a desperate attempt to unseat me. It'll never happen. It'll just divide their party that much more. Tweet by President Oscar Wellian

AND THEN IT WAS UPON us—the Democratic National Convention, held for the first time in over fifty years in Chicago, the location of one of the most controversial and divisive national conventions in Amberica's history. Of course, my network would cover every single second of it, with a large inventory of talking heads drilling down over every aspect of the democratic process.

In the next four days, some four thousand plus delegates would come together in an organized and thoughtful manner to make what they believe is the best choice for all the citizens of Amberica. And if you believe that horse crap, I have some swamp land to sell to you. This was guaranteed to be one of the most contentious conventions in the history of political conventions. Not only were there three nominees still statistically in the race, they were more diverse in their political leanings and platforms than ever before. Senator Schneider had rightly been labeled as the most centrist of the three, with Eloise Walker being a far left candidate with some hotly detested plans for reclaiming the country from the uber-wealthy and bringing back the middle class. But she didn't hold a candle to Angeline Tarkington, who some claimed was more of an anarchist than a politician. Her critics claimed she wanted to tear down the whole system and start afresh, something that Tarkington denied.

"We simply need to get real and tell some deep truths about how dysfunctional our politics have become and then start the hard, yet necessary, task of bringing it back in line with the First Principles so clearly outlined in our Constitution."

So, while I had a passing thought that this might be a good opportunity to start an extended leave of absence, I knew I couldn't live with myself, nor ever look Dottie or Cynthia in the eyes if I bowed out now. Instead, I dug in my heels and implemented the next part of my personal plan to make sure Tarkington and her campaign received their fair share of air time. I figuratively dug into my sack of favor chips, dumped the pile of them on the table and pushed them all to the center.

My colleagues hungrily accepted them, thankful to finally be even with me after all these years, but that still didn't feel like enough, so I started offering 'just call me anytime' credits, promising I would take over their show for a night on a minimum of notice. Of course, I couldn't do that for the other talk show hosts on the other networks, so I made other promises, ranging from a case of the finest whiskey to introducing one gentleman to my assistant, Cynthia. It began to feel like I was turning into a political pimp. Worse than that, I didn't care. There simply was too much at stake not to do whatever was necessary to make sure Angeline Tarkington got her share of air time.

Much to my surprise, many of my colleagues appeared much more open than I had expected. It finally dawned on me that since Ms. O's, Queen B's, and T.S.'s endorsements, the fringe candidate was no longer considered a wackadoodle, or if she was, she was now a much more interesting one. I began to regret being so liberal with my negotiations.

Meanwhile, rumors based on very few facts continued to spread that there was someone in the Democratic Party who was doing his own campaigning for one of the candidates, and that his candidate of choice was Angeline Tarkington. It was 3:00 in the morning when my subconscious mind somehow determined who this secret undercover "Angel" had to be. It woke me from a deep sleep, as I shot up in bed.

"Holy shit! Are you kidding me?" I turned on the light and reached for the pen and pad of paper I kept on the nightstand next to me. I started drawing a mind map of possible people and connections. It suddenly seemed obvious that my guess was very probably spot on.

My thinking went something like this. Angeline Tarkington and Ms. O go back decades, to when Ms. O had her own talk show, with Angeline being a frequent guest, along with hundreds of other celebrities like Queen B and T. S., and political figures, including a few Presidents, either as they were running for office or afterwards. The last piece that brought it all together was what my snitch had verified for me—that the person doing the dirty behind the scenes was from the Chicago area. It must be him. No one else fit the bill.

It had to be the former President, Barret Obaba.

"ARE YOU SURE?" STELLA asked. She cradled the cellphone between her shoulder and neck as she jotted down a note on a pad of paper. "Right. Okay, I'll let you know. Good work."

As she disconnected the call, Angeline Tarkington strolled into the room. "Who was that? Good news or bad?"

"That was Danielle. She was able to confirm the rumors we've been hearing."

Angeline stopped and stared at her campaign manager. "You're kidding, right?"

"Nope," Stella replied. "She's had no less than five of the former candidates admit that they've been approached with a direct request. If there's not a clear winner on the first ballot, they've been asked to use their influence to redirect votes to you."

"Holy..." Angeline left the expletive hanging. "And who is this masked marvel who's come to save the day? Do we know?"

Stella nodded again as she tore the sheet of paper from the pad and handed it to her candidate.

Angeline took it from her, then stared at her campaign manager after looking at the name on the paper.

"Holy crap! This is amazing."

Stella smiled and nodded. "This could just be the miracle we've been praying for."

Angeline walked over to her and the two of them embraced. "It just could be."

The two women continued hugging each other for another moment before Angeline stepped away and was once more all business. "Okay, let's be sure we're doing our part to bring this miracle home. Call all our delegates and make sure they don't waver on that first vote."

"We're on it," Stella said as she exited the room, her cellphone once more against her ear.

The First Ballot

I'VE SPENT MY FIRST term in office draining the swamp of so much corruption. We can't let the Dems back in to fill it up again. Tweet by President Oscar Wellian

WHEN IT BECAME EVIDENT that the Democratic National Convention would be the first one in over sixty years where there was not a clear winner from the start, the convention organizers decided to hold the first vote as early as possible. After all, they had only three days to determine who their candidate would be to run against, and hopefully defeat, President Wellian.

As expected, the first vote was split among the three candidates. What had not been expected was that candidate Tarkington had slightly more votes than previously calculated. *Could this be the first indication that the rumor is true*? I wondered, as I watched the final tally from my hotel room a couple blocks from the convention center.

What came next shocked everyone. The committee chair announced a change in the order of speakers that would follow the first vote. Former President Obaba, who had originally been slated to speak on the evening of the third day, after the candidate had been clearly determined, would speak within the hour. This announcement created more than a little stir among the delegates crowded together down on the floor.

I quickly finished dressing and rushed to the convention center. In the era of 'unprecedented' occurrences happening on almost a daily basis in the Wellian administration, this was one more such incident, except this time by the Democratic Party. I didn't want to miss it.

I arrived at McCormick Place and was once more amazed at its size and mass, being touted to be the largest convention center in Amberica. I showed my press pass and went through the thorough screening process to ensure I wasn't carrying a weapon or a bomb, then was allowed into the main hall, where I heard a restless buzzing still occurring from the recent announcement that the former President was due to speak within the next hour.

As often happens, it took longer than an hour for the President to appear, but sure enough, there he was on the stage, along with his lovely wife and a small entourage made up of other political big wigs with the Secret Service mixed in. A mounting surge of activity and applause followed as it became obvious to the throng of people that they were about to hear a speech from one of the most popular Presidents of all time, a speech that would go down in history, if for no other reason then when it was being delivered.

I managed to push and shove my way to within twenty yards of the stage, showing my press pass whenever someone took offense. Then, the committee chair stepped to the bank of microphones.

"My fellow Ambericans, it is my great pleasure to introduce a man who needs no introduction, a man who has shaped the course of human history, who has..." He paused as another man stepped forward and whispered something in the chairman's ear, who then quickly turned to look at the man he was about to introduce. A silent communication passed between them before he turned back to the mics.

"As I said, our next speaker needs no introduction, so without further ado, let us greet Chicago's favorite son, President Barret Obaba."

As might be expected, the convention hall went nuts, with banners from every State bouncing back and forth, and raucous applause and cheers that threatened to deafen us all. No one seemed to care that they had at least two more days of this madness. They let it all out for a good ten minutes, despite the President's efforts to subdue it. It had been a difficult three-and-a-half years for everyone in the hall, and they would not be denied the opportunity to let off some of the pent up energy and frustration.

Finally, with the assistance of the chairman's repeated gaveling for the room to come to order, and Barret's attempts to speak, the room quieted down. The tall black man stood and looked over the crowd with a smile of appreciation on his face, then he launched into his speech.

"We live in an unprecedented time with some of the greatest challenges in human history, not the least of which is our current President, who seems hell-bent on reversing all the good we managed to accomplish in my eight years in office."

The crowd yelled and booed at the reference to Wellian and his draconian policies. The President raised his hand and the room came slowly back to order.

"But I'm not here to speak of the past, but to address a rumor that has been circulating the last few days here at the convention and that has come to my attention." He paused and smiled. "So, let me clear this matter up so we can get on with the vitally important task of nominating our candidate, who will defeat Wellian in November."

Again, the crowd booed, and Obaba raised his hands for silence.

"The rumor has it that I've been going around behind the scenes talking to other Democratic leaders, including those candidates that have dropped out of the race, in an effort to persuade them to change their vote after the first ballot to a particular candidate. Can you believe it?"

There was a rumbling from the crowd that was quickly silenced by the chairman's gavel this time.

"Well, let me make this perfectly clear. The rumor...," he paused and scanned his eyes over the mass of humanity, "...is true."

The hall exploded in the loudest cacophony of sound produced by humanity I had ever heard. It was as if the noise typical of a National Football League game had been amplified ten times, and it went on and on for several minutes. The chairman and speaker were both powerless to subdue the crowd. Police and security stood at readiness in case any violence broke out, but with the exception of a few individual skirmishes that were quickly addressed, the mass of people seemed content to just yell and scream until they finally quieted, from fatigue as much as anything.

Finally, President Obaba stepped back to the microphones and continued. "I have been told that this speech and the actions that led up to it will be the end of my political career, but let's face it, my political career ended for all intents and purposes when I left office. It's time for me to pass the torch." He paused, waiting for the chairman to gavel the crowd back to order. "And there's one particular candidate that throughout this crazy campaign season has repeatedly and consistently stood for hope—the very thing upon which I built my two successful runs to be your candidate and President.

"So, let it be known today without question, the person I am endorsing, and whom I request you nominate as your candidate to run and defeat Oscar Wellian, is Angeline Tarkington, our next President of Amberica."

Needless to say, pandemonium ensued. After several minutes, the chairman tried to bring order to the chaos with his gavel, which could hardly be heard over the noise. Finally, in frustration, he slammed it down so hard he broke it, with the end spinning off the stage. He reached under the podium and pulled out a second one, raised it high above his head to strike the stand again, then stopped. He turned to the speaker and shrugged. They spoke a few words to each other before the chairman once again stepped to the podium, gaveled as loudly as he could, then yelled, "I call this meeting of the Democratic Convention adjourned until further notice."

THREE HOURS LATER, the convention was called back to order. Without any further speeches, the chairman called for a second vote, despite protest from several of the States that had voted initially for one of the other candidates. But even they knew that their protests would be insufficient to counter what had already occurred, so they allowed the balloting to take place. Angeline Tarkington received over sixty percent of the votes. The Democrats had managed to nominate their candidate by the end of the first day of their convention. The chairman thanked everyone for their effort and adjourned the meeting until the next day, when the new nominee would speak. Most of the people on the floor shouted and cheered, but there were also more than a few boos and catcalls, which the chairman chose to ignore.

Exit Stage Left

THE DESPERATE DEMS have just given the election to me with the nomination of Woo-woo Woman Tarkington who I'm now renaming as Woo-woo Witch. Onward with the remodeling plans. Tweet by President Oscar Wellian

THE SECOND DAY OF THE Democratic National Convention started bright and early at 9 AM with an assortment of business that no one really cared about, but that had to be conducted. Even the networks weren't interested and wouldn't pick up the coverage until 8 PM when the newly elected nominee would speak.

This gave Angeline time to prepare what she would say and to strategize on how to now bring the different factions together. It gave me the opportunity to sleep in and catch up on my rest. No telling what the next few days would bring. Of course, my boss had different plans for me, so when he didn't find me at my desk around 10 AM, he had Cynthia call me. I promised I'd get myself out of bed and in the office by eleven, and almost made it on time. The offices were surprisingly subdued considering such earth shattering news having just been made the night before. I began to wonder why Edward had insisted I come in. It didn't take long for him to answer that question. He called me into his office shortly before noon.

"What's up, boss?" I asked, as I sauntered into his office and dropped into the chair across from his desk.

He looked up from the paperwork he'd been working on, and from the look on his face, I knew I was in trouble.

"What's this I hear from the other hosts about your trading in all your, what do they call them?"

"Favor chips?" I offered.

"So, it is true!" He slapped his palm down on his desk.

Crafty old coot, I thought. I'd fallen right into his trap.

"Well, now, I didn't say..."

"You didn't need to say anything. I have you dead to rights. Do you know this could get you canned, and I don't mean just for a little while. This could end your career as a journalist. Trading in favors so that one candidate would get more airtime. What were you thinking?"

"I was thinking that our rigged system wasn't giving her any airtime and that I needed to, and could, do something about it. By the way, you did hear that the aforementioned candidate just won the Democratic nomination? She's the perfect candidate to take on Wellian. We can finally be rid of him and get this country back on course."

"That may or may not be true, but that's not the point," Edward replied.

"So, what is the point?"

"What happened to your journalistic integrity? That we're here to report the news, not help make it."

I stared at him across the desk long and hard before replying. "Are you kidding me? How can you say that after all the years we've done whatever we can to start as many shows as possible with 'Breaking News,' even on the days when nothing new was breaking? No, we and every other news channel have been about nothing more than how to survive the rating war for as long as I can remember. Journalistic integrity? It died with Walter Cronkite." I stood up and turned to leave.

"Where the hell do you think you're going? I'm not through with you."

I turned back around and smiled. "Maybe not, but I'm through with you. With you, with MSNBC and with this whole cockamamie lie that we've called 'the news'. No need to watch this space any longer because I won't be in it."

With that, I turned around and stormed out the door, exiting stage left.

Standing up for myself by quitting a job that I no longer believed in made me feel powerful and in control. That feeling lasted a good twenty minutes before doubt and regret set in. *Man, you really screwed yourself this time,* my inner credit agency informed me. *What are you going to do now? The rent, car payment, utilities are all still due the first of the month, not to mention that nasty habit you have of eating three square meals a day.*

Lay off, I countered. *I've got some money saved up for emergencies. Besides, I'll just get another job. No sweat.*

Yeah, what network will hire you? Oh, wait, no. You must mean a job at Mc-Donald's, right? No, no, silly me. You prefer Burger King.

This went on for close to an hour. Next thing I knew, I was standing at the top of the stairs that led down to The Dive. It looked as grungy and foreboding in the afternoon sunlight as it did in the middle of the night.

Go on in and have a drink. You can start pinching your pennies tomorrow.

It seemed like a good idea, so I started down the stairs, only to find Dottie standing in the doorway, her arms crossed in front of her like a bouncer.

"Where do you think you're going?"

"None of your business," I replied, as I started forward. "You're not even real, so get out of my way and out of my head."

"You poor baby," she purred. "You've had a hard day, haven't you? One drink won't hurt, will it?"

This change of attitude threw me off for a moment. "Yeah, that's right. Why don't you join me?"

She shook her head. "Nah, I think I'll let you self destruct on your own."

"Okay, suit yourself." But she continued to block the door. "Are you going to make me walk through you?"

She ignored the question. "Won't Bree be proud of you? Quitting your job and then falling off the wagon, all in one day."

"You leave her out of this," I snapped, but even as the words had come out of her mouth, I knew her sarcastic remark was just the opposite of what Bree would think. She'd be deeply disappointed in what I was about to do. I felt my shoulders slump as the air of outrage drained from me. "What would you have me do?"

Dottie uncrossed her arms and brushed her hair back in one of her classic moves I missed so much. "Go home, sweet boy. Fix yourself something to eat, listen to the new Democratic candidate's acceptance speech, then go to bed. Things always look better after a good night's sleep."

I nodded, then turned and climbed back up the stairs and slowly walked home. I took a long hot shower, fixed myself a sandwich and turned on the television just in time to watch Angeline Tarkington step onto the stage to a mixture of cheers and more than a few boos.

Angeline seemed to take it in stride. She let it go on for a couple of minutes, then held up her hands for silence. When the noise continued, she started talking in a normal tone of voice, which was easily drowned out by the hubbub. After about thirty seconds, when the crowd realized they were missing her speech, they quieted down, at which point she stopped speaking and flashed one of her most gracious smiles.

"Thank you. Let me start again. As I was saying, I so appreciate the opportunity to serve you and our fellow citizens of Amberica." As the crowd started to cheer again, she continued to speak with one hand raised for silence. "And it's now time to get to work. There will be plenty of time to cheer after we defeat Oscar Wellian, but let's not fool ourselves. It's time we started countering his long line of lies with some deep truths, and one of those deep truths is that Oscar Wellian is not the problem."

The crowd rumbled, and someone shouted. "Sure, he is."

"No, my friends. I beg to differ. Wellian is a byproduct of the problem. The real problem is that we've allowed our political system to be co-opted and undermined by the uber-wealthy elite, who have taken it over for their own purposes—namely, to put more money in their pockets. It's time we took it back."

This time everyone on the floor cheered and would not be stopped, despite Angeline's attempts to continue. She leaned over to the chairman. "I think I've made my point."

He nodded. When the crowd finally quieted down, Angeline continued. "So, with great humility, I accept the honor of your nomination. Now, onward to Washington, D.C." The crowd roared.

Part Two - Campaigning in Earnest

Post Nomination Night

IT HAS BEEN BROUGHT to my attention that with an Amendment to the Constitution I would be able to continue as your President for more than two terms. We still have so much work to do this may be a sensible course of action. Tweet by President Oscar Wellian

LIKE EVERYONE ELSE in the world, I was shocked beyond words by the nomination at the Democratic National Convention of Angeline Tarkington as their candidate to go up against Oscar Wellian in November. I was even more shocked when I received a call later that evening as I sat in my apartment with Rufus's head on my lap, lamenting my rash decision to quit my job.

"Good evening, Mr. Gramarly. This is Brasten Gramarly, right?"

"Why, yes, it is, but if you're trying to sell me a condo share or virtually anything else, I already have at least one of them." I started to hang up but the voice continued.

"No, Mr. Gramarly. This is Stella. Stella Romaine from the Angeline Tarkington for President campaign. Ms. Tarkington would like you to come see her tonight if possible."

"Why, hello, Stella, so sorry. I didn't recognize your voice." An image of her luscious figure flashed before my eyes, then was quickly replaced by her six foot three All Star running back husband. I shook myself back to the present.

"Angeline...I mean...candidate Tarkington wants to see me? Tonight?" *How can that be?* I thought. *She must have dozens of decisions that need to be made, like yesterday.* That included choosing her running mate, a decision that had ruined as many candidates out of the starting gate as had helped others.

"I would love to interview her as soon as it can be arranged..." I started to say, even as I realized I didn't have a show on which to carry out the assignment, but Stella was a woman on a mission and interrupted me.

"It has already been arranged. Can you be here in an hour?"

I checked my watch. 12:05 in the morning. "I'll be there in forty-five minutes," I replied.

"Perfect. I'll see you then." Beep.

Holy cow! This woman wasn't wasting any time getting the mainstream media on her side. But really, come to think of it, it made sense. I had interviewed her more than just about anyone else. Then it dawned on me that maybe she'd found out about my little conspiracy to get her on the other shows. Would she have a problem with that? I wasn't sure, but I started to worry anyway.

I arrived at the Ambassador Hotel a few minutes before 1 AM and was immediately escorted to the penthouse floor. Stella met me in the outer room of the luxury suite and thanked me for coming. "Ms. Tarkington is just finishing up a call. She'll be with you in just a minute."

I thanked her and she showed me to a seat. To make small talk and give me an opportunity to continue to gaze upon her beautiful face, I said, "It's been quite a night, hasn't it?"

"Yes, it has," she replied, offering me a bottle of water that I gratefully accepted. "And now the real fun begins."

I twisted the top off the water and took a long drink, then reached into my coat pocket and pulled out my steno pad and handheld recorder.

"Oh, those won't be necessary," Stella said, as she walked over and took them from me.

"They won't?" I asked. I stared at where she placed them on the table out of my reach. Suddenly, I felt naked without the tools of my trade. "But, I thought..."

The door to the next room opened and a lovely young woman stuck her head out and nodded to Stella.

"Ms. Tarkington will see you now." She motioned me to the door being held open by the assistant. I looked from Stella to the door and back again. I pointed to the pad and recorder. "Don't you think..."

Stella shook her head and pointed to the door. "No, not needed," she assured me. I slowly walked through the door to find Angeline Tarkington, the newly elected Presidential candidate of the Democratic Party, sitting in a chair next to the window, her cellphone on the table beside her. She rose and welcomed me with an outstretched hand. We shook, and I congratulated her on a well run campaign.

"Thank you," she replied. "Pull up a chair." She nodded to her assistant, who nodded back and left, closing the door behind her.

Angeline started to sit back down, but then changed her mind and walked over to the mini bar. "Would you care for something a little stronger?" she asked, as she reached in and took out a mini bottle of scotch for herself.

I thought about accepting, but then shook my head. Something told me I needed to keep a clear mind on this night of all nights. "No, this is fine," I replied.

She nodded, dropped a few ice cubes in a glass, and emptied the bottle into it. She took a sip, then sighed.

"I imagine you may be wondering why I asked to see you tonight."

"Well, I thought it was for an interview until Stella disarmed me." I smiled, but she didn't return it as she continued to speak.

"It's been quite a journey so far, and there are more miles to travel, and then even more miles after that." She gazed out the window into the night sky and at the city lights below. I wasn't sure whether the comment was intended for me or not, so I just sat there and listened.

She turned back to me. "Now the real work begins. Defeating Wellian won't be easy. His base is rock solid, and we don't know what outside influences from abroad we might have to deal with."

I nodded again. "Yes, you definitely have your work cut out." I glanced around, looking for a pad and pen, but found nothing with which to take notes. I didn't know what to do with my hands, so I juggled the water bottle from one to the other.

"I have some important decisions to make in the next twenty-four hours, not the least of which is choosing a running mate."

I nodded, suddenly feeling like one of those stupid figurines that used to sit in the back window of a car nodding incessantly. I stopped nodding and shrugged instead. Then, it finally dawned on me why she must have asked to see me. She wanted my input on who she should be considering as her V.P. Really? But wasn't that clear to her? It had to be one of the other twenty-four candidates she just ran against, probably one of the remaining top two. I racked my brain, but couldn't come up with any other legitimate choices. I opened my mouth to share that with her, then stopped, my mouth still open like an exotic flycatcher.

As I watched Angeline standing there with the night sky behind her, there was a glow, a highlight around her that I've never seen around any other person. Oh, I've read about people having an aura, but always discounted it as a bunch of New Age hogwash. Yet now, here stood the newly chosen Democratic candidate for President of Amberica, who would run against the man many considered to be the antichrist, glowing, positively glowing before me. Impossible, yet true.

I glanced down at the half drunk bottle of water. Had it been doctored with something? Was I about to start on a wild LSD ride that would end up with me lying in some gutter in the seamier part of Chicago? I returned my gaze to Angeline, who continued to stare at me, a frown forming on her face as the soft aura of golden light slowly faded.

"Are you okay?"

I realized she had asked the question for a second time. I shook my head. "What? Excuse me," I stuttered. "I've not had enough sleep these past few days."

"Tell me about it." She laughed. "Well, what's your answer? Do you accept?"

I shook my head harder this time and took another swallow of water. If it was laced with acid, I wanted to be sure to get my money's worth. "What was the question again?"

"Will you be my running mate? I need you on the ticket, and quite frankly, I won't accept 'no' as an answer."

I blinked several times and rubbed my eyes with one hand. I looked back at her and was relieved to see that she was no longer glowing. I was simply looking at a woman of slightly above average height, who was beginning to show her middle-age years. I could tell she was also tired and needed sleep. We all needed sleep. So, I blame my tiredness for my less than tactful reply.

"Are you freaking crazy? Having me on the ticket would be bloody political suicide."

Angeline cackled. "That's pretty much what my staff said." She took a sip of scotch. "And you all might just be right. Only time will tell, but I've made my choice, and for better or worse, you are it. You are the one. Well, technically, you'll be number two. I'm number one, unless something happens, of course. You know the drill, and now I'm rambling, so I'll stop and give you time to say 'yes'." She raised her glass to her lips and finished off the scotch, then strolled over to the mini bar and poured a second bottle into the glass before turning to me.

"Well, what do you say, partner? You know what they say about politics making strange bedfellows. Want to get in the sack with me?" She smiled sheepishly.

"You know I'm an alcoholic?" I asked.

"I know you have had your issues with booze," she said. "I also know you haven't gone on a binge in several months, right?"

I nodded.

"I also know you have a reputation as an incorrigible womanizer. You even made a couple passes at Stella before you found out who her husband was."

I nodded again. Dumb car ornament.

"I also have it on good authority you haven't slept with anyone since you started following the campaign. Rumor has it you have even been seen frequenting a church in your neighborhood."

"Now, that's a vicious rumor..." I started to say, then shrugged. "Yeah, maybe that's true."

Angeline walked over and stooped down in front of me so we were face-to-face.

"Here's the thing, and pay close attention," she said in a soft voice like a mother speaking to her child. "This isn't just about some election. Oh, it is that, to be sure, but it's so much more. This is about the transformation of a nation. Hell, a global transformation. And where does such a phenomenon start? With individuals—you, me, Stella, others. We all have pasts we're not proud of, but we're not our past, not if we are willing to learn from it and not be limited or defined by it. You and me? We are the poster children for that possibility, and that's why I need you on this ticket. It's also why I won't accept 'no'."

I continued to stare at her, dumbfounded by her request and feeling like a deer in the glare of an oncoming automobile. Finally, I found the strength to rise. I walked over and opened the door. "Stella, could we speak to you for a moment?"

Stella looked up from the papers she was pretending to study and nodded. As she entered the room, she glanced at me noncommittally and then to Angeline.

"Yes? Is there a problem?" Then she smiled, realizing how silly the question was.

"Will you talk some sense into her?" I asked.

Stella shook her head. "Sorry, I've already tried. Like we used to say in some personal development programs I led, I've broken my pickaxe trying to get her to reconsider." She paused before adding. "No offense intended."

"None taken," I replied. "But this is political suicide," I whined.

Stella shrugged. "Yeah, but it's her political future. As Angeline told me, it's been her trusting her inner guidance that's gotten her this far. She's not about to turn her back on it now."

As I looked from one woman to the other, I felt my shoulders slump in defeat. Evidently, Angeline picked up on the body language.

She stood up from the chair where she'd sat down when I'd gone for help. "Listen, I need someone who knows the game of politics, but who also has a different perspective than Stella here. Someone who knows the rules and how to get around them when necessary. That's you.

"I know we have a huge uphill battle," she continued. "The system is broken, yet still functioning. It's like the walking dead. I need your political savvy. So, political suicide or not, you're my V.P. Now, repeat after me: 'Yes, Angeline, it is my pleasure to accept.'"

My mouth was suddenly as dry as an arid desert. I took a swig of water and prayed that if this was an acid trip, I'd never wake up. I took one last look at Stella, and when it was clear she was not going to come to my rescue, I replied, "Yes, Angeline Tarkington, it is my pleasure to accept."

She stuck her hand out again and we shook."Oh, a couple things I need to clarify with you."

"Yes?"

"No more trading in favors to get me on other talk shows. I run a tight ship and such behavior is not acceptable from someone who's part of the campaign."

"Got it. No problem. The second item?"

"You'll need to resign from your position with MSNBC."

"Also not a problem. I already have."

"Really?" She looked surprised by my answer.

"Yes, we had a parting of the ways this afternoon."

"Well, okay, then we're all set."

"Let's kick some ass," I replied.

Angeline's smile disappeared as she glanced over to Stella and back to me. "Whoa, there. Let's watch the language. The last thing we need is losing votes because of a poor choice of words."

I nodded. "You're right. No more gutter talk."

She laughed and clinked glass to bottle to toast our new partnership.

"HAVE YOU TOLD HIM ABOUT the full disclosure press conference?" Stella asked, a few minutes after I'd agreed to be Tarkington's running mate.

"The what?" I asked. I didn't know what it meant, but I already didn't like the sound of it.

"Oh, no," Angeline replied, as she walked over to the mini bar, but this time she took a bottle of water out instead of scotch. "It slipped my mind. Why don't you fill him in while I go to the bathroom?"

"Sure thing. Leave the hard part to me," Stella quipped, but with a smile on her face.

"Always," Angeline replied, then excused herself.

After she'd left, Stella turned to me. "You may want to sit down for this next part."

"Really?" I asked, then decided to take her advice. My legs were already a bit shaky from what had already transpired.

"Okay, this is what's next," Stella started. Clearly what she was about to say didn't come easily. "There's to be a press conference a day or two after the convention closes."

"Okay, I understand. That's not all that unusual."

"No, but this next piece is, uh, a little unconventional. The purpose of the press conference is so that Angeline and you will have the opportunity to come clean about anything in your past that could be used against you by the opposing party."

"What? Are you kidding...You aren't, are you? Everything? Why, that could take hours just for my part."

Stella chuckled, then groaned when she realized I was serious. "Well, I'll work with you so you can bottom line it all. Cut out as much of the story as possible and just state the facts."

Angeline returned from the bathroom. "You know what they say: confession is good for the soul."

"Yeah, but I never bought into that malarkey," I replied. When I noticed Angeline's frown, I continued, "Well, of course, to each their own."

"A major part of my campaign has been that it's time we started telling some deep truths about our dysfunctional political system that has allowed someone like Oscar Wellian to be elected to the highest office of our land. Well, this will be part of that process. Telling our own deep, and sometimes dirty, truths."

It was my turn to groan.

"Have you ever been in AA?" Angeline asked.

"You mean Alcoholics Anonymous? Yea, for a little while, but then I dropped out. It just wasn't my thing. I mean, I know it's done great things for others..."

"Don't worry, I'm not trying to persuade you to go back," Angeline said. "You're familiar with their twelve steps, right?"

I nodded. "Sure."

"Well, just consider that this is our opportunity to take a 'personal inventory' and to do so publicly."

I stifled a second groan. Suddenly, being Angeline's running mate seemed like a really bad idea, and I hadn't been all that hot on it to begin with. "But why in front of the whole world?"

"Just think what we can accomplish in a relatively short period of time. We demonstrate to all Amberica that we're serious about the things I've been spouting off for months by 'walking our talk'. And, we knock the legs out from under our opposition. They won't be able to use our deep, dark secrets against us because we won't have any."

"You've got to admit, in a strange sort of counter-intuitive way, it does make sense," Stella added.

I put my head in my hands and tried to come up with some convincing argument I could use to get myself out of this situation. As I sat there, I heard Dottie's small, distant voice. *It won't be so bad. After all, you haven't killed anyone, or robbed a bank, or raped anyone, right? Right?*

Right, I assured her. *But I have been a closet alcoholic and devote womanizer. There have been many times I've either stretched the truth or downright broken it while doing my show.*

Is that all? If so, you have nothing to worry about. Just think what Angeline will have to confess.

Exactly! I almost leaped out of my chair, but managed at the last minute to restrain myself, instead looking up, trying my best not to smile too much.

"Wait just a minute. If we're both supposed to 'divulge everything', won't that mean you'll need to come clean about the mystery child you're reported to have had?"

Angeline and Stella stared at each other for several seconds before Angeline replied. "Yes, I will."

"Holy mother of...you're really serious about this, aren't you?"

"Absolutely," Angeline replied. "My country is on the verge of collapse from decades of corruption, deceit and lies. It's time we spoke the Truth with a capital T, and I'm willing to start it off." She paused, then added, "With or without my running mate. Will you be there by my side?"

I went to take a swallow of water, then realized the bottle was empty, so I crushed the plastic as I replied. "Yes, it'll be my pleasure." I sounded more convincing than I felt.

Full Disclosure

WOO-WOO WITCH TARKINGTON picks has-been talk show host, Grandpa Gramarly, for her VP? Are you kidding me? Watch this space, Grandpa. Tweet by President Oscar Wellian

AS I STEPPED UP TO the bank of microphones, I squared my shoulders and I looked out into the crowd as Stella had instructed me, with no smile and no frown. I was here to deliver a prepared list of my indiscretions, her words not mine, and then step aside so that Angeline could do the same.

I pulled the sheet of paper out of my jacket pocket, took a deep breath and started.

"I'm here today to fully disclose my indiscretions so you will know beyond a shadow of a doubt who you would be voting for in November to become your Vice President. This is one small step toward our ultimate goal to restore honesty, integrity and transparency to not only the White House, but all of politics."

I looked up as another series of cameras clicked, then I continued to read. "Number one. I have had a problem with alcohol consumption for a number of years. I was in rehab for the problem awhile back, but covered it up with a false report of being on a leave of absence. After returning from rehab, I became much more private about my drinking until about six months ago, when I stopped completely. I have been sober for these past six months."

I started to glance up from my notes, but then decided to forge ahead. *Let's get this over with already.* "I am known by many of my friends and colleagues as an incorrigible womanizer. I almost cheated on my wife several times while we were married. Thankfully, the women I hit on refused my advances. I have been single for the past three years following my wife's death from cancer." I paused to take another deep breath and to square my shoulders.

"I have not always been honest in paying my taxes. I am in the process of having my back taxes audited and will clean up whatever is necessary to be fully in compliance with the law."

I don't know how long I continued like this, though it felt like hours, and then finally I was finished. I looked at the cameras one last time and allowed myself a slight smile before turning around and walking off the stage as several reporters tried to ask questions despite the instructions that neither of us would be answering questions until later.

It was now Angeline's turn. She stepped onto the stage and took a moment to look around the room. "I am also here today to fully disclose things that I have done in my past. I will address the largest one first, the one that many of you have been investigating and asking me about.

"It's regarding the question of whether or not I had a child out of wedlock when I spent time in and around Haight-Ashbury when I was nineteen years of age." She paused, but I couldn't tell if it was for dramatic effect or to catch her breath. "The answer is, yes, I did have a child out of wedlock at that time. I carried the child to full term, and he was born on December 24th of that year, Christmas Eve."

Angeline paused again, and this time I could see her take a couple of deep breaths before dropping the bombshell. "Emory died on December 26th, two days later, from complications related to the delivery, and I entered a sanatorium for six weeks for treatment of postpartum depression after attempting to take my own life on December 27th. Stella, my campaign manager, will provide you with documentation for all of this at the end of the press conference."

She paused once more and reached for a glass of water. "I'm afraid the rest of my list isn't quite as long or interesting as my esteemed colleague's, but let me continue." She was very thorough with her list, even including how she'd regularly stolen money from her mother's purse as a child and later paid it all back three times over shortly after getting her own job. And like me, after she'd completed the list, she walked off stage without answering questions.

"WELL, IF THAT'S NOT a kick in the crotch," Honorable #1 growled to no one in particular, but Banyon responded anyway.

"Yes, sir. It certainly is, sir. Would you like me to get the other gentlemen on the phone?"

"Yeah, I guess so. Just give me a minute. How about a brandy in the meantime?"

"At 12:30 in the afternoon?" Banyon asked, then quickly continued. "Yes, sir. Right away." After bringing his employer the brandy, he placed calls to the other two men.

"I have them on the line, sir. Would you prefer speakerphone or video?"

"Oh, video, I guess. It's easier to tell if they're lying or hiding something from me."

"Yes, sir." Banyon clicked on the video screen and a moment later Honorable #2 appeared, but the other portion of the screen was taken up by Margaret, Honorable #3's nurse.

"He'll be right with you, sir," Margaret explained in a shaky voice. "He had a difficult night and is currently in the bathroom."

Honorable #1 groaned under his breath, but didn't say anything. Instead, he sat in his plush chair tapping his fingers on the armrest until Honorable #3 took Margaret's place.

"Well, did you see it?" Without giving them time to respond, he continued, "And more importantly, what the hell do we do about it? 'Bringing honesty, integrity and transparency back to politics'? How absurd is that?"

There was a long pause from the other two men before Honorable #2 finally spoke up. "Yes, I saw it, and I would advise we not over-react to it. It's just more of the typical Democratic rhetoric we've heard for decades. More importantly, so has the public. No one believes it anymore."

"Yeah, except she's backing up the rhetoric with action," Honorable #1 countered. "She fully disclosed everything that we were planning to use against her, and she had her running mate do the same thing. The public is not used to that."

"True," Honorable #2 replied.

"What about you?" Honorable #1 asked, pointing to the third man.

"I heard it, but from the bathroom. I'm not doing well, I'm afraid. My doctor is on the way over..."

"I got all that," Honorable #1 interrupted him. "Margaret told me, but what I need from you is a solution to this crazy woman who's threatening to upset everything we've spent decades building."

"Yes, yes, I understand. I did say we shouldn't under-estimate her. It appears I was right about that."

"Okay, you were right. Now what do you propose we do about it?"

Honorable #3 didn't answer for several seconds, but continued to rub the stubble on his chin as if in deep thought. Finally, he nodded as though he'd been having a conversation with himself and had come to some decision. "Smear her anyway," he replied in a weak, wavering voice.

"What?" Honorable #1 asked.

"Smear her anyway," Honorable #3 repeated, a bit more strongly. "Look, this was a clever move on her part, but ultimately it won't make any difference. We can still bombard the airwaves and social media with our own message. Hell, I bet our ad department can come up with some ways to use her direct quotes against her."

"He has a point," Honorable #2 spoke up. "We know the power of fake news and how impressionable the Amberican public is. This whole notion of speaking truth to power is highly overrated. Let's get our PR people on this. That's what we pay them the big bucks for, right?"

"Yeah," Honorable #1 replied, though there was something deep down in his gut that didn't feel right about this candidate, but since he didn't have any better strategy to use against her, he'd go along with an all out smear campaign. "Okay, let's move on this today."

Wellian's Celebration

CAN YOU BELIEVE IT? The Dems nominated Woo-woo witch Tarkington to run against me in Nov. I better watch out for her voodoo spells if I want another four years in the White House. I guess I can give the First Lady the go ahead for the refurbishing she wants to do. Tweet by President Oscar Wellian

WOO-WOO WOMAN TARKINGTON had a baby out of wedlock and now she claims it died two days later, but why should we believe her? I think an investigation is in order. Tweet by President Oscar Wellian

A DEPT. OF PEACE? REALLY? The only avenue to peace is to be sure you have the greatest military in the world and not be afraid to use it which I am not. Woo-woo woman Tarkington on the other hand wants to cut the military budget. A really bad idea. Tweet by President Oscar Wellian

WOO-WOO WITCH TARKINGTON thinks our government's primary job is to make it so everyone 'thrives,' her word not mine. So, she wants to open our borders and let in millions who are just barely surviving? Makes no sense! Tweet by President Oscar Wellian

Campaign Trail

From her own confession, Tarkington has given herself a new name. Woo-woo bitch. Tweet by President Oscar Wellian

CANDIDATE TARKINGTON and I hit the campaign trail almost immediately, with Angeline taking the lead and me remaining along the sidelines with Stella—a plan Stella and I agreed upon and finally persuaded Angeline to go along with.

"Sure, I've done my fair share of speaking in public," I told Angeline, when she questioned the move. "But from the other side of the mics and cameras, asking the tough questions and not being expected to answer them. Give me a few days to get used to the idea of being the second most powerful man...uh, sorry, I mean person, in the world."

"Do you really think the Vice President is that important?" Angeline asked.

"Well, no," I replied, "Not unless something happens to POTUS."

"Good. I was beginning to think I'd over calculated your political savvy. I'll give you a week to get settled in, but then I'll need you out stumping on your own. We've got a lot of ground to cover in a few short months. We can't have you on the sideline being babysat by Stella."

A vision of what it would be like to be babied by Stella flashed in my mind, but was quickly replaced by the image of her two hundred twenty pound husband pulverizing me.

You really are incorrigible, I heard Dottie say from somewhere deep inside me, but chose to ignore the obviously true statement.

"I promise to listen closely to everything you say and take notes. I'm a quick study."

"Good," Angeline replied. "I want to be sure our message is clear and aligned. At the same time, I don't want you to just parrot what I say. Find a way to say the same thing in your own words."

"Aye, aye, Captain," I replied, with a mock salute.

Angeline frowned, but didn't say anything further to me, instead turning to her campaign manager. "Stella, get Brasten a copy of our talking points so he can start studying them."

"Sure thing, Angeline," Stella said, then turned to me. "Come with me." As we walked off, she whispered, "Aye, aye, Captain? Where the hell did that come from?"

"My old military training," I replied.

"But you weren't in the military, were you?"

"No," I admitted. "You know me. I'm a lover, not a fighter."

Stella stopped and turned to me. "Okay, let's start right there. I've noticed that you don't seem to have much of a filter between what you think and what you say. On the one hand, it makes you quick on your feet. On the other hand, it sometimes leads to one of those feet being firmly planted in your mouth. I want you to start practicing slowing down just a bit. You are no longer representing just yourself, but also the Angeline Tarkington for President campaign. Eventually, if we're successful..." She stopped, then corrected herself. "...when we're successful, you'll be representing all of Amberica. Clear?"

I almost started to repeat 'Aye, aye, Captain', but stopped myself. *Might as well start being coachable*, I thought. "Yes, very clear."

Stella smiled. "Perfect."

It was the start of an amazing relationship, unlike any I had ever had up to that point. I learned a lot from Stella, not the least of which is how to grow close to a beautiful woman without constantly strategizing on how to get her in the sack. I discovered that not only did Stella have a beautiful face and body, she had an outstanding mind and grasp of politics. We made a great team, and the three of us spent a lot of long days and late nights on the campaign trail, especially in those first few weeks.

The best news of all was that the public was beginning to respond to our message, and it started to be reflected in two different places: the national polls and on Wellian's Twitter feed.

OSCAR WELLIAN LAY IN bed in a cold sweat after awakening from the same dream he'd had for the last three nights since learning that he would once again be running against a woman for his second term in office. *Where have all the Democratic men gone?* He wondered. *Are they afraid to run against me? Or maybe it's the Dem voters, or is that dim voters, that are afraid.*

He thought about that for another few seconds before pushing himself up in bed and reaching for his smartphone. He opened the Twitter app and started typing with his short, bulbous fingers:

Where have all the Democratic men gone? Are they afraid to run against me? Or maybe it's the Dem voters, or is that dim voters, that are afraid. He hit the Tweet button.

He thought about the upcoming election for a few more seconds and the conversations he'd had the past few days with Blowhard Honorable #1. *What is he so afraid of anyway?* he wondered. *Surely he knows my base will stand with me.* But Honorable #1 had insisted that he do his part by continuing the Tweet Storm, so he would. He started typing again.

Woo-woo woman is as much damaged goods as a candidate as the crooked one I beat so resoundingly last time. I look forward to four more years in the White House. He tapped the Tweet button again, then placed the phone on the night table before rolling over. Tweeting his thoughts out into the world to his enthusiastic fans was better than any sleeping pill he'd ever found. He closed his eyes and was sound asleep in minutes.

Bree

IF THERE WAS EVER ANY doubt that the fake news mainstream media is in bed with the Democratic party, has-been talk show host Grandpa Gramarly becoming their VP candidate is clear evidence. There should be an investigation. Tweet by President Oscar Wellian

THE HORRIBLE WEATHER across the northeast had forced the campaign into a ground game, and I found myself schlepping across the New York countryside tired and worn out from one stump speech after another. I leaned my head against the window and wished for the twentieth time I had thought to pack a pillow. I sat up to see if I could borrow someone's jacket, when I stopped and stared out the window. This stretch of road looked somehow familiar, like I'd driven down this road before, not once, but several times.

I glanced across the back seat to Paul, the Secret Service agent assigned to me, who sat up straight with his eyes far more alert than they had any right to be. "Any idea where we are?"

"Yes, sir," he clipped back to me, always the professional. "We're about twenty miles outside of Albany, on our way to Syracuse."

"Really?" I asked. How had I missed that we'd be covering this area of the State? Oh, that's right. We'd changed plans for the umpteenth time based on what the latest polls had shown. I'd given up trying to remember where I was going, though I had perfected what I was to say after repeating the same key points at least forty or fifty times. "How far behind schedule are we?"

Paul glanced at his watch. "Not behind, sir. Actually ahead. We're not due in Albany for another hour and we're only fifteen to twenty minutes out. Remember, we cancelled speaking in Kingston because of the projected low turnout and not having an indoor venue we could use."

I nodded as though I recalled it all, even though I was pretty sure I'd slept through that whole conversation. I made a snap decision. I leaned over and tapped the driver on the shoulder. "There's a road off to the right just ahead. I think it's US-45 or something like that. I want you to take it."

The driver nodded, but then countered, "That's not the most direct route, sir."

"I realize that. We're going to take a short side trip. There's someone I know who lives in this area with whom I need to talk. I want to be sure she's going to vote for us. Like Stella keeps saying, 'every vote counts,' right?"

"Yes, sir. Whatever you say. You're the boss."

Well, hardly, I thought, *but by the time the real boss finds out about this detour, it will be too late. Sometimes it's better to ask forgiveness than to ask permission.*

Twenty minutes later, our little entourage pulled into the parking area of Unity Center of the Mountains. Our vehicles were nearly the only ones in the parking lot, with the lone exception of an old Ford station wagon sitting in the spot designated for the minister.

Good, I thought. *She's here,* but that was followed by an immediate wave of fear circulating through my body. Suddenly the idea of dropping in unannounced like this seemed like a bad idea. I almost told the driver that we had the wrong address, or that the person I was hoping to see wasn't there, but stopped with my hand just inches from his shoulder when I saw Bree Taylor step out from the doorway and wave.

The fluttering of my heart cancelled out the wave of fear as I realized suddenly how much I'd missed seeing her. *Okay, here goes nothing,* I thought.

Go get 'em, tiger, I heard Dottie say. *Remember, you can be a gentleman when you want to be. After all, you won me over...eventually.*

She was right, as always. It was just the short pep talk that I needed to hear. I squared my shoulders and opened the door.

As I approached Bree, I felt my body's sensations of fear and excitement fight for control, and I almost fell and planted my face in the mud, but caught myself at the last moment.

"Well, look what the cat dragged in," Bree said, but with her typical winning smile that assured me she was joking, then added, "The next Vice President of Amberica, if I listen to my congregants, which, by the way, I do."

I felt my face blush from that last comment and suddenly I felt tongue-tied after weeks of wagging it around wherever I went. The situation only got worse as she reached out with both arms and hugged me, then gave me a kiss on the cheek. "It's good to see you," she said after she let go. "Care to come in and stay awhile?"

I nodded. "I'd love to," I replied. "I can only stay for a few minutes. We're on the way to Albany for a rally."

"Yes, I heard. I've been trying to finish up some paperwork so I could slip out to catch at least the last part of it, but I never expected a personal visit. Come. Come inside. I've just brewed a fresh pot of coffee if you're interested."

"That sounds great," I replied, still feeling the warm aftereffects of the hug and peck on the cheek, and with the musky fragrance of her perfume still tickling my nose.

Once inside, I watched as Bree prepared two mugs of java. She handed me one, then waved me to an overstuffed chair before sitting down across from me.

"And to what do I owe this unexpected, but welcome, visit?" she asked, before blowing across the steaming coffee.

I thought about trying some line like, "I was in the area anyway so just thought I'd drop in," but I'd been around Angeline and Stella too much to lie to her, so I opted for the truth.

"I've been thinking about you a lot. In fact, I did a little finagling to get these speaking engagements on the schedule so I could see you."

"Really?" Bree asked, with a surprised look on her face. "Well, I'm honored."

I nodded, though I wondered how honored she would feel if she realized how erotic many of those thoughts had been. "I was wondering if you'd like to have dinner with me sometime? I mean, you said if I'd get my life together, you'd consider it, and I'm unlikely to ever have my life any more together than it is now, so...." I left the comment dangling.

Bree smiled warmly, then took a sip of her coffee. "Why, yes. I'd like to have dinner with you. When did you have in mind?"

I suddenly realized I'd never figured she might say yes, and given my schedule, I wasn't sure how to answer her, but I just kept blundering ahead anyway. "How about tonight after I finished speaking, shaking hands and kissing babies?"

"Well, yes, that'll work. Just one question."

"What's that?"

"Do politicians still kiss babies?"

It was my turn to smile. "No, not really, but we make up for it by shaking that many more hands. So, it's a date? Is nine o'clock too late?"

"That would be perfect."

I felt my phone buzzing in my pocket. "That's probably my keepers. I better get going."

She nodded and we stood up together, and then a strange thing happened I can't explain. We were suddenly standing in the middle of her office in a warm embrace, followed a moment later by a lingering kiss.

Bree finally relaxed and stepped away. "Well, until tonight."

"Yes," I replied, suddenly flustered by the level of intimacy. "I'm looking forward to it. I'll be in touch to work out the details."

I started to turn towards the door, but she stopped me. "One second." She reached up and brushed a finger across my lips. "You had a little lipstick on you."

"Thanks," I replied, then turned to the door.

As I walked to the car, I heard Dottie say, *You sly dog. You've still got it.*

For once, I had to agree with her.

Part Three - Election Day Nears

A Video Arrives

THE FAKE NEWS MAINSTREAM media is once again colluding against the people of Amberica, focusing all their coverage on Woo-woo Witch Tarkington, but my people won't let them steal the election from us. Tweet by President Oscar Wellian

ANGELINE DROPPED THE hotel phone back in its cradle and turned to me. "That was Stella. She's on the way up. Seems she has something that came in the mail that she says we'll want to see. She called it a 'game changer.'"

"Really? Is that all she said? Not even a hint what it could be?"

"Nope, wouldn't say a word."

A few minutes later, there was a rapid knocking on the door, and Angeline walked over to open it. Stella rushed in, holding an envelope in her hands. "Oh, good, you're both here," she said, as she nodded towards me. "You won't believe this."

She walked over to the desk and opened Angeline's computer. "Don't worry, I've already had it checked for any viruses or malware. It's clean. Well, at least it's clean of any of that spyware kind of stuff."

What an odd comment, I thought, as I watched her put a disc in the side slot of the computer, but a few seconds later, it all made sense as I watched some of the poorest filmed porno tape I'd ever seen. The picture was blurry and granular, but even so, there was no mistaking who the man was sandwiched between two leggy women, one a brunette and the other a blonde.

"Why, if it isn't our esteemed President O. Wellian," I said, as I watched the two women pleasure the chunky older man, who lay in the middle of a round bed that looked like the setting of an old Rock Hudson movie. The three of us watched for three or four minutes as the scene became even steamier before Angeline finally reached over and shut the computer.

"Wait," Stella blurted out. "You haven't seen the best part yet."

"I've seen enough," Angeline replied. "We've heard rumors that such a tape existed. Any idea who it came from?"

Stella shook her head. "None, but it really doesn't matter. It's clearly Wellian and it's also obvious that neither of those women is his wife. Like I said on the phone, this is a real game changer. This will put you in the White House." She tapped the computer for emphasis.

Angeline stared at her campaign manager for several seconds before replying. "It might just do that if we used it, but we're not."

"What? You're kidding right? Someone is handing us the election. You can't look such a gift horse in the mouth. If Wellian had something like this on you, he'd use it. You know he would. Hell, I wouldn't put it past him to find someone who looks like you and make such a tape himself."

"Which is exactly why we're not going to use this one." Angeline reached over to the computer and removed the disc. "I want this destroyed."

Stella stared at her with a look of incredulity on her face. "It's our ticket to the White House. Imagine the kind of difference you can make once you're the President of Amberica."

"Yes, I know," Angeline replied. "And I plan to make that difference once we're there. This just isn't the way we're going to get there. I won't bring our campaign down to their level. We can win without compromising our own integrity."

Stella turned to me. "What do you think? We brought you on board for your political savvy. Talk some sense into her, will you?"

I shook my head. "Sorry, Stella, but it's her campaign. We all agreed she has the final say, and besides, I agree with her. This isn't the way to win."

Stella threw her hands into the air in exasperation. "I thought I'd finally backed a winner. My mistake. You'll have my resignation on your desk by the morning." And with that, she stormed out of the room, slamming the door behind her.

Angeline and I looked at each other, startled by Stella's pronouncement.

"She'll calm down and be back in the morning," Angeline assured me.

"I sure hope you're right," I replied. "We can win without that." I pointed to the disc. "But I doubt very much we can win without her." I pointed to the door where Stella had exited.

"You're right, there," Angeline replied, then, picking up the disc with both hands, she snapped it in half. "It's been a long day. Get some sleep. I'll see you in the morning."

I AWOKE THE NEXT MORNING to the song, *Ding Dong the Witch is Dead*, blaring from my phone next to my head. I'd set it as my special ringtone for Angeline's calls and now regretted it for the umpteenth time. I pushed myself up in bed and checked the time: 6:45. I groaned as I heard Dottie chide me with an *Up and at-em, Slugger* that I'd often heard when she'd been alive.

"Yes?" I said, as I answered the phone trying to sound as chipper as possible, but it came out sounding more like the croak of a hungover frog.

"Stella just called, and she's on the way over. Can you come up?"

"Sure," I replied, as I swung my legs to the side of the bed. "Did she say whether she's reconsidered her decision?"

"No, and to be honest, I was too afraid to ask. I figured if she's still planning to resign, you and I would have a better chance of changing her mind in person than over the phone."

"Good thinking," I replied, as I stumbled towards the bathroom. "If nothing else, we could tie her up and not let her go until she reconsidered," I said glibly, then immediately regretted it. All that work Stella had done with me and it was already wearing off.

"Not funny," Angeline said. "I've already considered it."

"I'll be right up," I said, then ended the call so I could piss in private.

I decided to forego a shower and instead sprayed an extra dose of antiperspirant under my arms and splashed on some cologne just in case. Remembering how Dottie often accused me of having the worst morning breath in recorded history, I did take the time to brush my teeth and use mouthwash. I quickly changed into a dress shirt and slacks and grabbed my shoes and socks, putting them on as I waited for the elevator to arrive. All in all, I made it to Angeline's room in just under fifteen minutes, and was relieved to find I'd beaten Stella there.

I nodded to the security officer standing outside her door before knocking on it. Angeline must have been waiting for me on the other side because she opened it immediately. "Good, it's you," Angeline said, obviously relieved to see me. "Come inside and let's plan our strategy."

"Strategy?" I asked.

"What are we going to do or say if she still plans to quit the campaign?"

"So, tying her up is off the table?" *There I go again,* I thought, but was relieved to see her smile.

"For the moment it is. Let's see what else we can come up with. Do you care for a cup of coffee?"

"Please."

She walked over to the cart where her partially eaten breakfast lay and poured a cup of coffee from the carafe. "So, any other ideas?" she asked, as she handed the cup to me.

I'd been thinking about the question since receiving the call, but my brain seemed unwilling to boot up this early in the morning. I took a sip of coffee, only to discover it was lukewarm at best.

"How long have you been up?" I asked. I'd noticed as I came in that Angeline looked rougher than I recalled ever having seen her.

"All night," she replied, confirming my suspicion. "I tried to sleep, but I couldn't get my mind to turn off. I tried everything I could think of, counting sheep, meditating...nothing worked. I just don't know what I'll do if she resigns."

"Okay," I replied. "We just won't let her. If she says she's quitting, we'll decline her request."

"Yeah?" Angeline said, a look of doubt on her face. "And then?"

"Well, then we'll trust that one of us will have come up with something intelligent to say after that."

"Really? That's the best you've got?"

I shrugged. "I'm afraid so. You have a better plan?"

Angeline shook her head. "Not a one."

There was a knock on the door. "That must be her," Angeline said. She squared her shoulders and walked over to let Stella in.

As she entered the room, my first thought was, *Damn, she looks worse than Angeline. Is that a good sign?* At least it meant she'd had a tough night trying to decide what to do.

"Coffee?" Angeline asked, sounding more casual than I would have been able to pull off.

"No, thanks," Stella replied, then, noticing me sitting on the edge of the bed, added, "Good. You're both here. I'll make this quick and clean. I've given what happened last night a lot of thought. Stayed up most of the night, in fact. And I've decided...," she paused for a moment, "...that you were right. It is your campaign and it would be wrong for us to lower ourselves to that level."

I heard Angeline release a deep sigh and started to do the same, but Stella wasn't finished. "However, we need to get something straight if I'm to continue on the team."

"What's that?" Angeline asked.

"As things now stand, we will lose to Wellian. Not only lose, but it's likely to be a landslide in his favor. I don't say that to be mean, but as you've often said, Angeline, it's time to tell some deep truths and this is one of them." Stella looked from Angeline to me and back to Angeline, letting the words sink in before continuing.

"So, we have to pull out all the stops, while maintaining a high level of integrity, honesty and transparency. This is not going to be easy. It will be the hardest thing any of us has ever done. Winning a presidential campaign is never easy. Doing it honestly? Well, I doubt anyone has ever even tried that before, so we're definitely breaking new ground. If we win, we'll be making political history."

"When we win," Angeline corrected her. She walked over and gave Stella a hug, and once again, I suddenly found myself magically transported across the room and hugging them both. After several seconds, we separated.

"It's time," Angeline declared. "Let's make some history."

THE NEXT SEVERAL MONTHS were some of the most intense, hectic and stressful of my life. I felt like the last kid in a long line playing Crack the Whip, and that on any given day, I might be flung off into space by the frenetic pace we all kept. These weeks were also the most exhilarating and fulfilling, as I watched our poll numbers slowly climb until we started to see reports of the race being "too close to call". I never knew four words could make me feel so good, at least four words that had nothing to do with women or sex. But I digress.

Such reports only served to urge us forward to the next speaking engagement, the next social media live stream or the next fundraiser. It also served to keep me awake on nights when I really needed my sleep, wondering what life would be like if we actually won and I became the Vice President of Amberica. But during the day, I was too busy on the campaign trail to give it much thought.

"It's official," Stella said one morning when the three of us gathered together in another hotel room outside of St. Louis. She dropped a copy of the morning edition of the *New York Times* on the table in front of us. I gazed at the headline:

Presidential Campaign Too Close to Call

"That's great!" Angeline said, after reading the first few paragraphs. "This will serve to encourage our Angels to work that much harder for us, both our mortal ones and the spiritual ones around us."

By this time, I was used to hearing such comments from her and Stella, though I'd also noticed that they rarely made such references unless we were alone with no press or public. When I'd asked Angeline about this, her reply was simple and direct: "No reason to encourage the press about my being a 'wackadoodle' or 'Crystal Queen.'"

It seemed to work. In the past several weeks, all such mention had disappeared except in the most conservative news outlets. The rest of the world was definitely taking us seriously.

"You know, we could really do this," I said, as I picked up the paper to look for the sports section.

"We are going to do this!" Stella and Angeline both exclaimed, virtually in unison.

"Sorry," I replied, stepping away from them to avoid any further wrath. "I know—no doubts or second guessing. Straight ahead to the White House."

"Exactly," Stella agreed. "Now, put that paper away and let's get to planning how the next set of headlines can read: "Tarkington Forges Ahead to Victory.'"

We Know What to Do

THE FAILING NEW YORK Times continue to spread fake news against me, claiming incorrectly that the election is close. So untrue and unfair after all I've done to help Amberica. Tweet by President Oscar Wellian

HONORABLE #1 DISCONNECTED the call with his three 'groomsmen', an archaic term he used to describe the two men and one woman who were still in the running to eventually take his place on the Triumverate, though not necessarily in the number one position. It was a well-honed system that kept the reign of power intact from generation to generation.

He glanced at his watch. Just enough time to relieve himself before he met with the other two world leaders to decide what to do about this latest challenge—the 'wackadoodle' Angeline Tarkington, who had turned out to be anything but a nut job. As he stood in front of the toilet waiting impatiently for his prostate to relax enough to let at least a small stream of urine pass, he thought about how they might have approached this situation differently. What had they missed about her? *Perhaps I should have listened to #3 more keenly,* he thought. Honorable #3 had warned them not to discount her appeal to the general public, but who would have thought she'd be able to actually make a run for the presidency?

He paused for a moment to focus on the task at hand, trying to relieve his bladder. He really should schedule a visit to his doctor, but he already knew in his gut that it wouldn't be a simple visit, pick up some meds, and all would be relieved. No, his doctor, who was one of the foremost physicians in the world, would insist on a rectal exam, followed with blood tests, X-rays or even a cat scan, all to learn some bad news that he already knew. He was getting old and his systems were slowly wearing out. *Ahh, hell. It'll have to wait until after the campaign.*

He zipped up his pants, washed his hands and grabbed one of the linen towels next to the sink. He then walked to the conference room, where he found Honorable #2 and Honorable #3 waiting for him.

"Good afternoon. Thanks for coming. I'm sorry I'm late. My 'groomsmen call' took a little longer than anticipated."

"Not a problem," Honorable #2 said. "We know how important those calls are."

"And what a pain in the ass they can be, as well," Honorable #3 added. "Still, none of us is getting any younger."

"That's for sure," Honorable #1 agreed, as he made his way around the table to his seat. "I thought you Big Pharma guys were going to take care of that. Invent some Fountain of Youth pill or something."

"Maybe we will, maybe we will," Honorable #3 chuckled, then coughed. He waved his nurse away before she had a chance to intervene. "I'm afraid most of our time right now is spent inventing new diseases for some of the drugs our chemists have developed, but don't have a way to market."

"Well, how about getting some of the chemists going on a 'forever youth' pill, will you? We're running out of time," Honorable #1 replied. "Now, on to some real business. What are we going to do about this?" He picked up the remote and clicked on it. The far wall lit up with a giant image of the *New York Times* front page with the headline:

Presidential Campaign Too Close to Call

The other two men stared at the screen while Honorable #1 studied their reaction. Clearly, they'd either seen the paper or heard similar reports. Neither man showed any surprise at it. Their silence also suggested they didn't have a ready solution to the problem either. The three men stared at the screen for over a minute, as though they expected the answer to their problem to magically appear. When it became evident that no such miracle was going to happen, Honorable #1 reached over and pressed the intercom button. "Let Chef Andre know that there will be two additional guests for dinner tonight." He clicked off the intercom without waiting for a response and stared at his two comrades.

"We're not leaving until we have a clear plan. Is that understood?"

The two men nodded.

"So, let's start brainstorming. How do we intervene and make sure, in the couple weeks we have before election day, that this appraisal by the *Times* turns out to be one more bit of Fake News that the *New York Times* printed?"

After several more seconds, Honorable #2 spoke up. "We can increase the negative ad campaign we have going, especially in the swing states."

Honorable #1 reached over to the control panel and pushed a button and watched as the video screen split in half, revealing a large whiteboard behind it.

With a nod from his boss, Banyon stepped forward with a large felt marker and started writing Honorable #2's suggestion at the top of the board.

"Okay, next idea," Honorable #1 said, offering no opinion of the first one. They all knew the rules. No criticism of anyone's ideas was allowed during this phase, even though Honorable #1 found himself biting his tongue to keep from saying how stupid and ineffective he thought more negative ads would be.

"Come on, gentlemen. Let's have it. Remember, there are no bad ideas at this point. What else can we do to stop Tarkington from stealing the election from us?"

"Why not let Wellian debate her? Maybe he can intimidate her into making some major blunder," Honorable #3 suggested. Banyon wrote it on the board while Honorable #1 again bit his tongue.

The process continued for close to an hour, with the white board filling up with suggestions, none of which seemed to Honorable #1 to be a viable solution, either individually or even collectively. *But, that's okay,* he told himself. *That's often how the brainstorming process works. You have to get the bad ideas out of the way to make room for the one good idea that's been hidden by the bad ones.*

Several more minutes went by and Honorable #1 was about to call a recess, since his tiny bladder was once again alerting him to the need to pee, when Honorable #3 cleared his throat. "There's one idea that isn't up there on the board," he began. "You know, I remember back decades ago when I was a green-as-could-be groomsman. Hell, I was barely twenty. It was in the late sixties and the Triumvirate of that era was in jeopardy of losing power. We all remember that time, even if we simply learned about it later."

He paused to look at the other two men. "It took some radical action to right the ship. Personally, I think they may have overcorrected, but that's just me. The point is, aren't we in more or less the same situation? We know what we need to do, but we're dancing all around it. Why? Could it be because this time, the problem we're facing is a woman? Or are we simply too scared to do what we know we need to do?"

The question hung in the air for almost a minute before Honorable #1 finally broke the silence. "Are you suggesting what I think you're suggesting?"

Honorable #3 slapped his hand down hard on the table. "See! You're even afraid to say it, so I will. Kill her, gentlemen. Assassinate her. End this travesty before it's too late. It's why we're here in these seats. We've been groomed to make the tough decisions and then to follow through with action." He took a long breath and slowly let it out. "I move that we proceed with such action without delay. Time is of the essence and our hold on this country is at stake." Honorable #3 sat back in his seat and finished his inelegant speech with a fit of coughing.

When he finally calmed down, Honorable #1 spoke up. "We have a motion on the table that we take action to have Angeline Tarkington assassinated. Is there any need for further discussion?" But before anyone had a chance to speak up, he continued. "In that case, all who are in favor, raise your right hand." He slowly raised his own and watched at the other two men followed suit. "Okay, the motion carries unanimously. We will adjourn for fifteen minutes. Be thinking about which of our folks would be best to get this done. We'll finalize the details when we reconvene."

MAGDALENE ANDREA SAT in the outer area of her principal's office, waiting for him to get off the phone. When the light on the secretary's phone blinked off, she glanced over to the secretary, who smiled and nodded.

"You can go in now, Maggie, and don't worry. He'll understand your need to take a few days off. I'm already calling substitute teachers to find someone who can take over your classes."

Maggie returned the smile and stood up, straightened out her floral dress and strolled into Principal Harrod's office. "Good to see you, Maggie. Please, have a seat. What's up? I hope all your students are behaving themselves."

"Oh, yes, the little dears are all fine. I'm afraid it's my great aunt who's not doing well. She's the oldest living member of our family, and I'm afraid it may be her time."

"I'm sorry to hear that," the principal replied. "And so, I'm guessing you'll need a few days off to visit her?"

"That's right," Maggie replied, wringing her hands in mock apprehension. Harrod was like putty in her hands, always had been, and today would be no exception. She'd already booked her flight and packed her bags. This was all just to cover her bases and make sure she had a job to come back to after the assignment.

"Is there anything else I can do?" Harrod asked. "Please, leave your great aunt's address with Janine so we can send her some get well flowers."

"Oh, that's so sweet," Maggie replied, then added, "If you could say a prayer for her, I'd really appreciate it."

"Most certainly, and you take good care of her. We'll hold down the fort here."

Maggie stood up, thanked him again and left. As she walked down the hall, she pulled out the burner phone from her purse. She'd kept it there for the last nine months since she'd purchased it from Walmart, shortly after her last job. She dialed a number and waited for someone to pick up on the other end. She waited to hear the code word before saying, "I'm on my way to Los Angeles as directed. I'm on the job. Consider it done."

She exited Will Rogers High School, and as she walked by the dumpster on the way to her car, tossed the phone in it. She looked forward to caressing her semi-automatic sniper rifle after so many months. It would be like two heart-starved lovers finally getting back together again.

The Last Rally

IF YOU WANT TO KEEP the criminals, thieves and rapists out of our Amberica, you must vote for me on Tuesday. I will keep you safe. Tweet by President Oscar Wellian

"I'VE BEEN CALLED MANY things during this campaign, including a witch and a bitch, so I figured it was time for me to embrace them both." Angeline stood on the stage of the Pacific Amphitheatre and gazed out at the throng of cheering supporters. She was dressed in a purple witch's outfit and wearing absolutely no makeup, as the Secret Service had insisted for this Halloween rally.

I glanced at Stella and she smiled back at me. We had discussed at length what Angeline's opening statement should be for this last campaign rally. What she had just spoken had not even been on the short list, but we had both come to accept, and even expect, that from time to time Angeline would go off script. After all, she had an amazing ability to read the crowd and deliver the perfect line.

It had been a torrid last couple of weeks as poll after poll reported that this presidential election would likely be one of the closest in recent history, even rivaling the election of 2000, when "hanging chads" in Florida led to such chaos that the winner finally had to be decided by the Supreme Court.

With each reported poll, Wellian's Tweet storms grew more blustery and personal, with Woo-woo Woman being replaced by Woo-woo Witch and then later Woo-woo Bitch, all of which was duly noted by Angeline, yet only inspired her to be even more confident on the campaign trail.

My gaze moved from Stella's smile to the massive crowd that filled to overflowing the Pacific Amphitheatre as they cheered for their candidate. That's when I noticed something was amiss. *Where are the Secret Service...* I was still processing the thought when the glint of light from one of one of the distant towers drew my attention. It would be sometime later before I realized the spark of light must have been the sunlight reflecting off of the sniper's telescopic sight, but by then the damage had already been done. I heard the lone crack that sounded like a car backfiring and watched in horror as Angeline stumbled back as if in slow motion. Then, Stella ran toward her in an effort to catch her and took the next two bullets in the back. The two of them fell to the floor of the stage. Time seemed frozen while I stared in shock as the two women I'd grown to love over the last few months lay motionless, with the crimson circles growing on Stella's back. Then, time and motion resumed as I realized that Angeline was trying to struggle out from under Stella's inert form.

"The candidate has been shot!" I shouted, as I finally made myself move in Angeline's direction and saw a growing blood stain on her left shoulder. *Shot, but still alive. But how?* I wondered. It would be another minute, while pandemonium grew around us, before I realized that, beneath her witch's costume, Angeline wore a bulletproof vest that had partially protected her from the sniper's bullet. It would be much later, when the authorities reviewed the video, for us to learn that it had taken the combination of the vest and Stella's quick action to save Angeline's life, but cost Stella hers. The second and third shots had been slowed by Stella's body and had lodged in Angeline's vest.

I stooped down to protect Angeline in case the assassin wasn't finished, and placed the heel of one hand firmly on her shoulder to slow the bleeding until help arrived. She grimaced as the shock of pain grew more intense and through tight lips said, "Sure didn't think I'd ever need this darn thing." With her right hand, she tapped the top of the bulletproof vest that had just saved her life.

I nodded. "Lie still. Help is on the way," I said, though in truth I didn't know if anyone was coming.

"How's Stella? Is she okay?" Angeline asked.

I glanced over at Stella's still body, lying in a spreading pool of blood. I didn't know how to answer that question, so I repeated, "Just lie still." I reached into my back pocket, pulled out a handkerchief and placed it on her wound, then glanced around to see two men in medic uniforms, each carrying a black bag, rushing towards us. *Finally,* I thought, even though it had been less than a minute since the first shot had been fired.

When they arrived, I stepped out of the way so they could do their work. One of them attended to Stella and the other began working on Angeline. A half dozen police officers were now surrounding what had become a crime scene. The officer in command looked at me. "Did you see anything?"

I nodded and pointed in the direction I'd seen the glint of light. "Over there at the top of the tower. I saw a spark of light like a reflection."

He nodded, then got on his radio to pass along the message to the rest of his team. "Shut it down," I heard him say as he moved away. I turned my attention back to the two medics. The one that had been attending to Stella looked up and shook his head, but didn't say anything.

"What can I do?" I asked, feeling as helpless as I have ever remembered being.

"You can help make a path so the rest of our team can bring in the stretcher," replied the medic who was placing a temporary bandage over Angeline's shoulder.

"How bad is it?" Angeline asked.

"Not that bad," the medic replied. "The bullet went straight through the vest and your shoulder but didn't hit any vital organs. You'll be sore as hell for a few days, but you should recover fully."

"Good to know," Angeline said. "I still have a presidential election to win."

The medic nodded and smiled. "Well, you sure as hell have my vote."

"Mine, too," the other medic added.

I thanked both of them for their care and for their votes. I had a funny feeling that this event, tragic as it was, might be just what Angeline needed to take her on to victory.

Two stretchers arrived moments later and Stella and Angeline were placed on them. They covered Stella's face with a sheet and I knew beyond any doubt that she'd no longer be a part of the campaign. I also knew she'd been willing all along to give it her all, and she surely had. It was now Angeline's and my job to be sure her death had not been in vain.

Election Day

WHILE WHAT HAPPENED at Pacific Amphitheatre was a real tragedy, don't let it sway your vote come Tuesday. I had nothing to do with it, though I suspect the dark forces of the Dems may have. Tweet by President Oscar Wellian

IMMEDIATELY FOLLOWING the shooting, the news cycle whirled into high gear, with video of Angeline's last campaign rally appearing on every station, along with the assurance that, while the Democratic candidate had been wounded, she was expected to fully recover. The story went on to say that it had been the heroic action of her campaign manager, Stella Romaine, that had saved her life. The news hounds even caught up with Stella's husband, Dallas Romaine, as he was preparing to board a flight from Washington, D. C. to Costa Mesa to make arrangements for his wife and to do whatever he could to "make sure Stella had not died in vain."

So, yes, Dallas and I finally did meet, and I have to admit that, despite the horrible circumstances that had brought us together, I was more than a little nervous about shaking the burly guy's hand. I needn't have worried however. It became clear within the first minute that Stella had refrained from ratting on me.

Despite the heavy security of the rally, somehow the shooter had managed to escape, though one spent cartridge was found at the tower location that I had pointed out to the officer. Evidently it had rolled away and in the rush to escape, the shooter had failed to find it. A state-wide manhunt ensued, but I paid little attention to any of that. Instead I focused on two things: making sure Angeline received the best medical care possible and trying to sort out the epiphany I'd had while on the stage looking down at my two fallen comrades and thinking that both had just been brutally murdered in front of me.

But that second matter would have to wait. Like Angeline had said while lying bleeding on the floor, we had an election to win, and a little over seventy-two hours to go. So, despite receiving advice to the contrary by her medical team, Angeline insisted on speaking to the public from her hospital bed on Sunday afternoon, less than a full day since narrowly escaping the assassin's bullets.

Angeline tried to persuade her doctors to let her stand in front of a podium in one of the hospital's meeting rooms, but that's where the doctors and I drew the line. She'd talk from her bed or she'd wait at least until Monday afternoon and then see if she was strong enough to leave her room.

"Besides," I told her when the pronouncement was made, "Let's face it. You speaking from your hospital bed just a day after almost being assassinated by your opposition—now, that's great optics."

Angeline stared at me. Despite having received a blood transfusion, her skin's pallor still troubled me, but not as much as the frown that formed on her face. "I know one of the reasons I wanted you on the ticket was for your political savvy, but really, you should know me better than to think I'd be concerned with the optics. In fact, that is exactly why I would prefer to stand behind a podium like a regular candidate."

"But you're not a regular candidate, not anymore. If you ever were. Let's not forget that when you started this campaign, you were considered the 'fringe candidate', and that was one of the nicer terms used. There was also wackadoodle, not to mention witch and bitch, as you shared yesterday just before you were shot and almost killed. If it hadn't been for Stella's bravery..." I stopped, as I noticed Angeline tearing up. There were other wounds besides just the one to her shoulder and her bruised ribs that also needed to heal. I suspected the emotional wounds would take far longer.

"I'm sorry," I said. "I'm floundering here. We're both barely keeping our heads above water without Stella's wise counsel."

Angeline nodded. She glanced around, looking for a tissue. I reached over and handed her one. "Okay, we won't overplay that you're speaking from your hospital room. We'll have the cameras focused on your face and keep it short and to the point. The main thing is that we want to assure the Amberican public that you are alive and out of danger. Okay?"

Angeline nodded. "Agreed."

"Is there anything else for now?"

"Just one thing. I'll be going to my polling place to vote on Tuesday. Would you like to go with me?"

I started to object, then closed my mouth and nodded. I'd heard that note of conviction before and had finally learned not to argue against it.

IT TURNED OUT I NEEDN'T have worried about whether Angeline could pull off a press conference so soon after being shot. She did, in fact, keep her statement brief and on point.

"I want to thank everyone who has prayed for me. I feel your healing energy coursing through me, and I want to assure you that this will in no way interfere with my ability to carry out the responsibility of the office if you are so generous as to elect me to be your next President. I am healing just fine, and it's now time for us to take the next step in healing our country from the fear and hate we've had to endure these last four years. Please, everyone who is eligible to vote, if you haven't already done so, come out on Tuesday and make your voice be heard. Thank you."

MONDAY TURNED OUT TO be the most hectic day of my life as all the last minute actions of the campaign fell on my shoulders, and I realized just how indispensable Stella had been to the campaign. Luckily, she had trained a small team of Angeline's Angels, who picked up many of Stella's responsibilities and kept me out stumping for every vote possible.

No one on the campaign was taking anything for granted, including Angeline, who spent hours on the phone orchestrating last minute details with the campaign offices of the key battleground States.

I had taken advantage of early voting in New York, so I was free to accompany Angeline on Tuesday to her polling station, where we were met with a wave of reporters, who joined in with the other voters in applauding her as she stepped out of the SUV, followed closely by her entourage of Secret Service agents.

She waved to them before entering the building, where she insisted on standing in line to vote, claiming, "Today, I'm just an ordinary citizen taking advantage of my right to vote. Tomorrow? We'll see."

It was a brave effort that cost her dearly. By the time she'd finished casting her vote, she was obviously tired and pale from the effort. As she exited the voting booth, she leaned over to me. "Get me out of here."

I held her by one arm as I signaled to one of the Secret Service agents to alert the driver. Entering the backseat, I shouted to the driver, "Straight to the hospital, pronto."

He nodded and gunned it. As we roared down the highway, Angeline leaned over and placed her head on my shoulder.

"I think I overdid it today," she whispered to me.

"That's okay. It's all in God's hands now," I said, repeating one of her favorite lines.

Her closeness reminded me of the revelation I'd had on the Pacific Amphitheater stage. *Maybe it's time I came clean about it*, I thought, but when I glanced down at her, she was already asleep.

Angeline spent the rest of the day sleeping while I stayed on the phone with our various campaign offices and tried unsuccessfully to stay away from the TV coverage. I gave up the effort around 7 PM when the first polls on the east coast began to close and the early results dribbled in.

The accuracy of our exit poll results were soon verified. The voter turnout was destined to be a record breaker, with over 156 million casting their ballots, in part due to a surge of young voters, who typically stayed home on Election Day, coming out en masse, along with African-Americans and women, all three strong Democratic blocks.

I returned to Angeline's room to find her sitting up in bed eating a cup of yogurt and watching the news.

"How are you feeling?" I asked, as I sat down in the chair that had become my primary residence these last few days.

"Much better," she replied, taking a spoonful of yogurt and offering it to me.

"No, thanks. Much too healthy for my taste. The early returns are looking promising."

She nodded. "Still early though. Remember what happened last time the country voted for President."

I remembered all too well. It had looked so promising for the Democratic candidate up until around 10 PM, when the key battleground States came in, all in favor of Oscar Wellian. Many citizens had gone to bed early, assured that the Democratic candidate had won, only to awaken to learn about the late night upset.

History would not repeat itself on this night. Angeline's lead continued to grow as the night wore on and by 10 PM, it was clear there'd be no last minute rally for Wellian. NBC, CNN and MSNBC declared Angeline Tarkington the winner within minutes of each other, with Fox News reluctantly following suit less than an hour later.

We heard a clamoring of noise outside our room as the hospital staff and many of our own supporters celebrated.

"Well, Madame President, you did it," I said, as I rose from my chair and walked over to her bedside.

"We did it," Angeline replied with a broad smile on her face. "Now the work really begins."

"That's for sure," I agreed. "But can we hang out with the accomplishment for just a little bit?"

"Sure thing."

I bent down and gently hugged her, trying not to touch her wounded shoulder. I realized I probably only had a minute or two before someone would barge in from outside, and it would then be a long time before we'd be alone again so, on the spur of the moment, I decided now was the time to share my revelation.

"Something happened to me, too, on that stage the other day," I began, not sure what was about to tumble out of my mouth, but forging ahead anyway. "When I saw you go down from the assassin's bullet and then Stella right after, I thought you'd been killed."

Angeline nodded, but didn't say anything.

I tried to swallow, but my mouth was so dry, I found it impossible, so I just kept letting my emotions form the words.

"In that moment, I knew..." And that was as far as I got before the door flew open and a flood of people entered the room to congratulate the next President of Amberica.

OUR CAMPAIGN VOLUNTEERS teamed up with the hospital staff to transform the cafeteria into a celebratory venue complete with Tarkington2020 signs and a mass of balloons and streamers. Meanwhile, Angeline's doctors and I teamed up to insist that she be wheeled down to the basement level, although we did concede she could stand at a podium this time to deliver her acceptance speech. Then it would be straight back to her hospital bed to continue her rest and recuperation. Cynthia had sent for "Makeup Mindy" from MSNBC to be sure Angeline looked as healthy and vibrant as possible. Of course, Angeline resisted at first, calling it a deception, but she finally relented when Cynthia pointed out that she'd worn makeup throughout the campaign, with the lone exception of the night she'd been shot.

"Okay, point well taken," Angeline conceded. "Pile it on." Mindy nodded and went to work. She finished by straightening the sling that supported Angeline's left arm.

We suddenly realized that in the rush of the last few days, no one had looked far enough ahead to prepare an acceptance speech.

"Don't worry about it," Angeline assured me. "We can trust Spirit will provide the right words. She's done pretty well up to now."

I nodded as I helped her into the wheelchair and pushed her in the direction of the elevator. As the door slid open, she turned to me. "Let one of the Secret Service guys take over from here. "You're my VP. You should be beside me, not behind me. Optics, you know."

I smiled at that last little jab and relinquished my spot.

The hallway to the cafeteria was filled with well-wishers who had been thoroughly scanned for weapons of any kind, so it took us several minutes to make our way to where the celebration was already well underway. Before entering the cafeteria, I helped Angeline out of the wheelchair and Mindy took one last moment to be sure her makeup was perfect, with just the right amount of blush and lipstick to create the appearance of a healthy President ready to lead the country for the next four years.

As I leaned over to give Angeline a reassuring hug, I whispered in her ear, "Game on," then added, "May Spirit speak through you."

She returned the hug before squaring her shoulders and stepping into the room to the sound of *God Bless Amberica* and a rousing chorus of cheers from her supporters. I walked next to her, lightly holding her elbow, as much for moral support as anything. I needn't have been concerned. She was well prepared for this moment. A vital spirit had infused throughout her body.

She stepped behind the podium and waved to everyone, igniting an even louder, enthusiastic cheer that continued for several minutes. Finally, Angeline raised her right hand to ask for silence.

"Dear friends and citizens of Amberica, thank you, and a special thanks to all of you who came out to vote for either candidate!" The room erupted in cheers and Angeline waited patiently for it to stop. "I am committed to being everyone's President and I realize it will take time to win your trust." The cheers started again and this time Angeline raised her good hand in an attempt to silence the crowd.

"I also want to thank my running mate, Brasten Gramarly, as well as my campaign staff and the hundreds of volunteers who worked so diligently for so many months." Before the crowd could cheer again, she continued. "I especially want to take a moment to express my eternal gratitude for my campaign manager and true friend, Stella Romaine, who gave her life for this country, and I dedicate this presidency to her memory." The crowd applauded and this time, Angeline let them voice their love for the fallen hero.

"We've much work to do in the coming weeks and months to begin the process of healing this country and so I ask that we start now. Please join me in thanking President Wellian for his efforts..." Angeline quickly hushed the few boos that started with her next line. "And I ask you to join me in forgiving President Wellian for any misguided efforts and transgressions. We are all imperfect human beings on our own journey to perfection. I will no doubt make my own share of mistakes and will need your forgiveness as well.

"At the same time, let's not mistake forgiveness for condoning a person's imperfect actions. Stella Romaine was killed by an assassin's bullets and I was wounded." She glanced down at her left arm supported by the sling. "I assure you, citizens of Amberica, there will be a thorough investigation, and if it is de-termined that President Wellian was involved, he will be held to account."

The crowd cheered as Angeline Tarkington, the new President-elect, exited the microphones and slowly made her way out of the room and back to her wheelchair.

Back in the room, Angeline was only too happy to return to the comfort of her bed, where one of the nurses checked her wound and her vitals. The nurse then turned to assure me that everything was fine.

"Thank you," Angeline spoke up. "Could you give my Vice President and me a few minutes alone?" The nurse and the two Secret Service men nodded, then exited.

"What's up?" I asked. "Is there anything wrong?"

"No, not at all. Everything is right with the world at the moment," Angeline replied with a smile. "I was just wondering. It seemed like you wanted to share something with me earlier but were interrupted. What was your revelation back on that stage?"

A wave of trepidation passed through me and suddenly my mouth was once again dry as a desert in the midst of a sand storm. "I...well, I'm not sure this is the moment or the place," I stammered.

"It was okay a little while ago. Come on, out with it. We can't start out the presidency with secrets between us, can we?"

I shrugged. It didn't seem like such a bad idea at the moment, but then I knew she was right. I had to get this off my chest, so after a quick glance at the door, I started again.

"As I stood there on that stage looking down at the two of you, with Stella lying on top of you and all the blood...I thought for sure you both had been killed." I took a deep breath before continuing. "And in that moment, I knew beyond a shadow of a doubt that you are the woman that I love above all others, and that I've loved you from the moment I met you, even though I wouldn't allow myself to admit it."

The startled look on Angeline's face should have stopped me, but instead I felt compelled to continue. I heard footsteps from outside approaching again.

"So, will you marry me?"

Angeline's gaze flitted to the door and back to me. "What? Being Vice President isn't good enough for you? You want to be the First Gentleman, too?" Angeline asked.

I nodded, then bent over and kissed her just as the door opened. A moment later, I heard Cynthia's voice behind me say, "Are you kidding me?" As I turned in her direction, I heard Dottie chuckle. *You've definitely still got it.*

A Message from Brad Swift

(a.k.a. Orrin Jason Bradford)

AS AN INDIE AUTHOR I know just how important readers are. Without people who enjoy reading, authors are pretty useless. Oh, I know I enjoy the thrill of writing the *next great American novel,* but that's really not enough. I need readers like you who enjoy reading my stories. So, thank you. I sincerely appreciate your taking the time to read *The Fringe Candidate.*

Perhaps you would enjoy some of my other books and stories. If you'd like to stay up to date on new book releases, special discounts, and my occasional giveaways, you can join my **OJB's Amazingly Awesome Readers Group**. Just go to my author's website and blog where you can also download a free copy of one of my other books: www.wbradfordswift.com

There's one last thing you could do if you would be so kind. Go to your favorite online bookstore and leave an honest review of *The Fringe Candidate.* Honest reviews are really important to help other readers like you know which books to try next. And thanks for being an amazingly awesome reader.

Brad Swift (a.k.a. Orrin Jason Bradford)

P. S. And check out some of my other books on the next page.

Other Books by Brad Swift

VISIONARY FICTION (As Orrin Jason Bradford)
The **FreeForm Science Fiction series**

- *FreeForm: Crash (A prequel)*
- *FreeForm: Beginnings FreeForm: New Birth*
- *FreeForm: Reborn FreeForm: New Power*
- *FreeForm: Resumed FreeForm: New Earth*

Short Story Anthologies

- *Fantastic Fables of Foster Flat*

- *More Fantastic Fables of Foster Flat (volume 2)*
- *Hunt Along the Iron River & Other Timeless Tales*

Babble (Book one of the Cosmic Conspiracy series)
(As W. Bradford Swift)
Spacehoppers
Zak Bates Eco-Adventure Books

- *Dominion Over All*
- *Endangered*
- *Ghost Elephant*

Amberlin series

- *Amberlin: Divine Destiny*
- *Amberlin: Awakening*

Visionary Non-fiction

Life On Purpose: Six Passages to an Inspired Life
Spiral of Fulfillment
Purposeful Prosperity
Learn more at www.wbradfordswift.com[1] & Author.to/wbswift

Porpoise Publishing
Flat Rock, NC 28731
www.wbradfordswift.com
Library of Congress Cataloging-in-Publication Data
The Fringe Candidate (The Amberica Series Book One)
Brad Swift
ISBN: 978-1-930328-92-1
1. Visionary Fiction 2. Political Intrigue 3. Alternate History

Printed in USA
First Edition

About the Publisher

Porpoise Publishing is the imprint of indie author W. Bradford Swift who also writes under the pen name of Orrin Jason Bradford. It is best known for publishing visionary fiction--stories that entertain while also inspiring readers to imagine greater possibilities for their lives.

www.ingramcontent.com/pod-product-compliance
Lightning Source LLC
Chambersburg PA
CBHW021047130626
46552CB00005B/2048